I0617592

EFEMENA
FICTION

Kraftgriots

Also in the series (FICTION)

EFEMENA

FICTION

Gift Foraine Amukoyo

kraftgriots

Published by

Kraft Books Limited
6A Polytechnic Road, Sango, Ibadan
Box 22084, University of Ibadan Post Office
Ibadan, Oyo State, Nigeria
℡ +234(0)803 348 2474, +234(0)805 129 1191
E-mail: kraftbooks@yahoo.com;
kraftbookslimited@gmail.com

© Gift Foraine Amukoyo, 2018

First published 2018

ISBN 978–978–918–510–8

= KRAFTGRIOTS =
(A literary imprint of Kraft Books Limited)

All Rights Reserved

Cover design by Uchay Joel Chima

First printing, July 2018

Dedication

For
Mr and Mrs Godwin Amukoyo;
Adeniyi O. J. Adewole (Arc),
Amukoyo Jimoh Nyerovwo,
Juliet Amukoyo and
Hycinth Egedi,
My inspiratory heroes

Prologue

Enitekiru's body was on mystical fire. She burned and continuously shouted, "Erharen! Erharen!"

Her neighbours could not see the invisible flames but the elders knew she was being scorched. They summoned a priest who divined the cause to be an offense against her father-in-law. Enitekiru confessed to the crowd, that she had prepared meals for him while unclean.

Enitekiru had been married for a while and knew about the taboos of her husband's community. Fejiro Ohakpoma had not failed to list the customs and traditions of his community to his wife whom he had married from an entirely different community with unfamiliar customs. It was forbidden in his clan for a woman in her menstrual period to cook or serve her father-in-law food in his son's home. Out of vindictiveness for his unannounced arrival, which had made her cancel a trip to the neighbouring village's masquerade festival, she prepared his meals and served him. If she made her monthly flow known, her father-in-law would request for scent leaves which he would dip into clean water and sprinkle all over the house. This is a process of cleansing the environment as a woman was considered impure during this period. She was to desist from entertaining until the curse ceased.

"Abomination! She has desecrated the laws of our ancestors," an old woman said and spat on the ground.

Enitekiru was quickly taken to the village, Uriamukpe, where her husband was resident for a family meeting. She recounted her deed and Pa Onoharhese was dismayed, but vowed he could not let his son's wife die. He demanded that a drink be bought by some members of her family which he used to pray and put some in her mouth. Immediately the gods were pacified, she came alive and called for food. She consumed the garri she was given in a big-sized calabash like a glutton. When she gained enough strength, Fejiro took her back to their home at Amukpe. He could not bear the discreditable way members of his clan stared at him like he had not lectured his wife on the clan's customs.

✳   ✳   ✳   ✳   ✳

"Oso Onoriode, please I need money to buy a new Hollandaise wrapper for the forthcoming women town's meeting."

"Enite, but I have pleaded with you to wear the wrapper for the last meeting so that I can pay Aruegodore's school fees with my next salary."

"Are you saying my wrapper and ornaments are not important? Aruegodore's books are your priority than your wife's image in public eh?"

"You know that is not true. You always make me proud with your glowing attires at occasions. Biko, let me offset Arue's school issues, his final exams are approaching."

Enitekiru hissed and left the bedroom where her husband was counting some coins. She fumed all the way to the farm; "that Aruegodore will not allow me enjoy my marriage with his study books and fees demands."

"Women can never be satisfied with their needs, they always desire pleasure at all cost." Fejiro shook his head at his wife's fading murmur and tucked the bag of money underneath his clothes box. Enitekiru stretched her legs and peeped through the splits of the bamboo window to see where her husband would hide his money. She later went in, took some coins out of the bag and hid it in Aruegodore's only pair of shoes, fixing three pence in each. Enitekiru's evil ploy to cause misfortune for her brother-in-law brought misery upon her. She set Aruegodore up for a crime he did not commit and he was labeled a thief. Fejiro chased Aruegodore away from his house and refused to pay the fees for his final year examinations.

✲ ✲ ✲ ✲ ✲

Months later, Enitekiru could not conceive. The pregnancy was accompanied with excruciating pains. The oracle revealed that the child was resentful. Through the oracle, Enitekiru's unborn child said if she did not confess, both of them will die. Neighbours gathered from near and far because words travelled, Enitekiru had been pregnant for fourteen months. "Woman, you need to confess so that you will be free from this labour of yours," the priest said with his teeth tightly clenched to lemon grass leaves.

"Orodena, I do not understand you. I have nothing to confess." She heaved and sighed, as another contraction wracked her body.

"Yes, you do and you shall speak, for your daughter warns you to, else you die with the baby in your womb." He spat the chewed leaves.

"Omotemena." Enitekiru looked around confused.

"You shall give birth to a girl. Speak woman before it is too late. Speak now of your evil deeds else your death will be miserably recorded in history. Surely the oracle will spill your wicked act after your demise."

Weeping, she said, "Orodena, bear witness to my condition. I am already at death's wit and it toys with my senses. Right now, all I can see is the seventh heaven and underworld. Biko, recount this woe fleeting my memory."

The priest retrieved a brown bottle from his leather bag made from elephant skin. He took a thin swallow of gin and spat hard that it splashed about.

"Think, woman! Think of past evil. Remember your deeds: money, greed, boy, shame. All these have happened under this roof." He sat on the floor legs crossed and threw seven white cowries on the floor. They rolled like sleek dices, sprawled and rested between her thighs.

"Arue-go-do-re," she said breathlessly.

"Speak," he urged her.

She looked up to her husband who stood at her side. "I am sorry my husband, please forgive me. I stole that money not Dore, it was never Aruegodore. I did not want him to stay in our house or attend higher school. I did it so you would not sponsor his education." She began to cry.

"You brought disgrace upon my household. You tried so much to shred us. When will you stop these mischiefs in my family? Some time ago, it was my father, now you have made me commit grave injustice towards my brother, Enitekiru, my own blood," Fejiro blurted out in pain and anger.

"Oshare, this is not the time to scream if you must save your wife. Run along and get the offended person this minute," the priest said to Fejiro with his eyes wide open, his intimidating eyeballs dancing like wavering fire.

"At once, Orodena." Fejiro made to run but a neighbour held him back.

"Let me go and fetch the young man, you may not be able to handle your bicycle in this state." Fejiro nodded in agreement and let out a hefty sigh.

Aruegodore, who had gone back to the village, arrived and Enitekiru apologized to him. He accepted and was happy to regain his honour.

"Go now, look around; anywhere you find faeces of fowl, touch it with the big toe of your right foot and scoop some. Remember; once you have taken it, do not look back and do not allow your right foot touch the ground. The child knows you have not forgiven her mother, if it touches the earth. She would assume you still carry hate in your heart. It would mean you still loathe her parent and for that reason, she would not be delivered,the priest instructed." Aruegodore went in search of the fowl's faeces and carefully hopped back.

"The viridity of a rabbit should not be addled as it feeds delightfully on carrots. Now woman, open the mouth you told lies with. These faeces shall cling to your tongue, for the hen does anything within her power to protect its chicks from preying eyes. The dung shall rub off the stains you smeared on your brother in-law. After that, you will blossom from your womb." The priest spoke while he pranced around Enitekiru. She opened her mouth and the priest instructed Aruegodore to place the waste on her tongue. Forthwith, she gave birth. The baby spewed forth, and the crowd marveled. The priest lifted the newborn and gave midwives broad plantain leaves to wrap her. He raised her and shouted:

"Anaborhi! Anaborhi! Anaborhi! Omotekoro! Omotore!"

He returned the baby, packed his divination tools and with backward movement, exited the house.

Fejiro was displeased with Enitekiru's ways. He severed his intimacy with her since all she did was cause troubles in his family. Fejiro asked her to leave for some time, that she could come back when she was able to mend her bad ways. Enitekiru refused to go back to her father's house; she claimed she could not leave her ten-year-old son behind.

Six months later, Fejiro took young Enatomare, from Uriamukpe, as second wife. Enatomare was married at the age in her village, parents, guardians, and kinfolks feared for the reputation of maidens, as many were getting fraught. The elders decided it was more honourable for them to be married at tender ages,

10

than birthing baseborn in one's parental home. She had six older sisters, a year apart in their ages. They all had children after Uwadah dance festival, a time that marks the beginning of a raining season as a bountiful period to nurture what had been sown. This anticipated period of reaping rewards of hard labour, capital, strength and time devoted to farmlands came with celebration ending on the gambol mat for some.

Udaze, Kevwe, Oyoma, Enatomare's older sisters were lucky. Udaze married Jekwu her lover who travelled with her back to his roots, Igbinaboe town of Ijakiri land. Kevwe was married off to a foremost palm wine tapper Udezi a drunkard who was also the jest of Omullala kingdom. While Oyoma became the sixth wife of Chief Arubayi, the rest became a pack of layers in their father's compound, giving birth to chicks of different breeders. When Enatomare came of age to tell a river from the ocean, she observed that water could be fresh or saline. That in life, odourless liquids could also taste like bile.

As a child, she rarely complained of hurts or expressed displeasures. Somehow at each footing in life, she was satisfied after being cared for in whatever measure. If fed palm kernels for three square meals, or handed down tattered clothes to wear, she was always appreciatively contented. She grew up a reclusive lady, but turned out altruistic after realizing that in the African society, a child is parented by many.

People described her as a woman with a fragile heart, though decisive with a warrior's mind. She never could bother anybody but herself. She tasked her abilities to any length that seemed right to accommodate her family and society. People randomly said, Efemena, her daughter, took after her traits.

Enitekiru jealously vowed to make Enatomare's marriage miserable. She kept poison in her husband's food and blamed the new wife who had prepared and served the meal.

After the burial of Fejiro, both women appeared at the family's personal shrine. Enitekiru appeared first, before Irahun, and ate ewieun. She became raving mad by daybreak, ran into the bush and hung herself. Her madness was hot with Irahun's fire. Her people cried she was innocent, but many did not doubt that she soiled her hands, for they had witnessed some of her deeds in the past.

Aruegodore Onakpoma's dream to scale through his studies and marry his university sweetheart was shattered. He was committed to marry his late brother's widow, Enatomare, shared to him as custom in their culture and being the eldest amongst his brothers, it was inescapable for him.

❦‖ *One* ‖❦

Aruegodore and his family were in the village for his late father's burial. Being the Okpako amongst his father's children, Aruegodore was informed that Pa Onoharhese had given up the ghost; he died as the oldest man in the whole of Elume community. It was an abomination for anyone to hear about his death before his first-born. Aruegodore must be the first to know and give his consent for his father's death to be generally announced. Aruegodore was to perform all traditional rites according to the customs of the clan despite being a deacon. The general overseer of his church counseled him to go ahead in order to avert retributions that would trail his generations if he failed to comply, that he should willfully give to Caesar what is Caesar's, and to God what is God's. The people of Uriamukpe reverence Oghene, as the supreme deity of their land. The other divinities were the Erivwin which is the cult of the ancestors. The dead are believed to be alive, and are revered as active members who watch over family affairs. They also believed in the duality of man; that man consisted of two beings: physical body – Ugboma, and the spiritual body – Erhi.

Erhi declares man's destiny and directs the self-realization of his horoscope before he incarnates. Erhi also controls the total wellbeing of man. Oghene's lordship and supremacy confirm the seal on foreordination set by Erhi.

In Erivwin, man's destiny is ratified and sealed. In transition, the final journey into the supernatural realm, they believe the

Ugboma decays while the Erhi is indestructible and turns to join the ancestors in the spirit realm and combine forces to protect their descendants.

Sequel to his illness, Pa Onoharhese drank gin with his forefathers. He knew that the grim reaper had begun its journey to his threshold. He solemnly asked his children not to deposit his body in the morgue. He said, " The docile restroom of a western deep freezer will cool my quest for vengeance if I die by the fruit(s) of a woman." It was Pa Onoharhese's wish to be buried no later than three days, in order to take up arms against his murderers if the need arose. His corpse was not deposited at the morgue. It was traditionally preserved with a concoction of herbs at home. The clothes Pa Onoharhese wore at his death – wrapper and shirt, Aruegodore took to the stream and washed with native soap made of liquid extracted from burnt green plantain peels and kernel oil. Those clothes were used to embalm him for two days in his private parlour.

Aruegodore was instructed not to look backward as he went to and fro the stream. When dried, he wore the undersized clothes, sat on a very small stool facing the shrine as some elders told him the words to recite for Irahun, the burning god of his clan.

He wore a cap and was given a headgear to tie around his neck as he spoke to the ancestor: *Osomo, as I make these sacrifices to you, I beseech you join our ancestors in the world beyond to pray for your children who are remaining on earth. On failing, the benefits of these sacrifices shall not be honorary to you; your soul shall not rest in peace. So bless us Oso.*

In the shrine, ewieun was served as customary. Roasted goat was cooked and the head was served to everybody inside the parlor. Each child and close relatives of the deceased were given a piece of meat and asked if he or she knows anything about Pa Onoharhese's death. This rite is usually dreaded because it is merciless, if one is found guilty after consumption, death is the ultimate consequence.

Efemena watched this fascinating ritual process through a recently fixed sliding window. She was relieved when her father consumed the ewieun and took his seat comfortably. He did not look like a man capable of hurting a fly. "Meeena! Meeena!"

Efemena turned to see her mother waving a broad pawpaw leaf and beckoning her to the backyard. She stepped daintily on leveled empty shells of imekpe–periwinkles–meant for remodeling the outer walls of the house. Reaching her mother's side, Efemena shaded her eyes from the sun with a pawpaw leaf.

"Izu, I did not realize it was you that called." She tried to slap a buzzing housefly that perched on her nose.

"What happened? It is so unlike the way you call my name, are you alright?"

"Come with me into the bush, I am so pressed." Efemena's mother squeezed her face like someone in labour.

She did not bulge. "What are we going to do in the bush?" She slapped another fly, this time killing it. She ground it to the earth, as though that would wipe its species from existence.

"Biko mo, my bowel is on riot."

"Why is there no toilet in this house? How can a bungalow with six bedrooms not have a kitchen, bathroom, and toilet?" She walked behind her mother who hastily led the way.

"You complain too much, Mena; here you should come to terms with village settings. Despite the little wealth of your grandfather's children, he adamantly refused to renovate his house. He forbade anyone to tamper with a house he built in his proud youth."

Mena's mother went further into the bush until she found a spot not littered with dried faeces. She dug a hole in the soil with a bamboo stick.

"Oh, Izu," Efemena drawled. Enatomare positioned her buttocks at the hole. "I hope you have some antibacterial drugs inside, this is highly infectious."

Enatomare sighed wearily from her daughter's complaints.

"Tell me, Mena, since we came here, have you not relieved yourself for once, where do you defecate?"

"I am yet to poo."

"Are you kidding me?"

"Definitely not," she shrugged.

"But how is that possible? I mean, for three days we have been here?"

"Yeah actually, I pee when I bathe in the makeshift bathroom, while some prescribed drugs I took have prevented me from defecating."

"Mena, you have to be careful with orthodox medicine. They could have terrible side effects."

"No side effects, Doctor Fola assured me that much," she said.

She smiled when her mother gave a knowing look.

"You have the privilege to bathe in closed doors. In the past, girls your age had their bath outside, at morn and eve." Enatomare grinned when she read utmost disbelief on her daughter's face.

"That was to tease you; but seriously, girls between the ages of twelve to seventeen years had their baths in front of their various houses." She wiped her buttocks with the leaves, and wiped with tissue paper afterwards. Efemena could not help it, she burst out laughing uncontrollably.

"Izu! Did you have to do that? I mean what is the point of bringing a tissue when you were going to use greens? I thought you are very comfortable with village life."

Her mother grinned and said, "I just felt the urge. You see, Mena, village life can be so fun." She looked into the bush as if she could vividly see her past.

"What could be fun about one wiping buttocks with leaves? Oh stop, that is so hilarious!" She continued laughing.

"It's better in this clime. Do you know, Mena, back in the days; the two methods of cleaning buttocks were either with a stick parents erect close to the makeshift bathroom or with pawpaw leaves because of their soft texture. Then at school, students would wipe their bums on pit latrine walls." Enamatore stood up, readjusted her wrapper tying it more firmly.

"Really? Many bums to a stick! Oh my goodness! That is so interesting. Go on, tell me more, Izu."

"With all pleasure, I will, Mena. Some minutes will do. After that, I would have my bath in our humble bamboo bathroom." She laughed heartily as the prospect of telling her daughter stories of the past filled her with joy. Efemena followed her mother as they made their way to an Udara tree.

"Mena, did I tell you that before your grandfather died, he had his baths outside? The best stage in life is when an individual's brain is a tabula rasa; an age of innocence and a pure inhabitation. At that age, one is oblivious to dangers of men. I remember Ebelebe, an old jovial woman. She used to have her bath in front of her house. If children go to peep at her, she would open her shriveled buttocks and flash her ass at them. She wriggled her waist like the Udje dancer that we feared it would break in halves."

"Oh my goodness," Efemena laughed.

"Yes, Mena, whenever she does that, we would take to our heels; but she had identified our faces. She would come to our houses later and seek permission from our parents for farm labour; to till, plough, and plant seedlings for the better part of the day. She set aside Wednesdays to weed. You need to see how sore our hands turned out. We became shy to extend hands to admirers, the blisters were irritating."

"Very funny woman," Efemena smiled.

"Yes, Mena, she was adorable. Her husband was just the perfect match for her; the couple were an intriguing terror to youngsters in the village. Before people learned how to dig pit latrines, when bushes were developed into factories, houses and town halls, some oil companies ran pipes through lands. The host communities were warned not to wander into bushes to avert spillage or explosion because some persons would carry along kerosene lanterns. Therefore, each house had a big bucket they defecated in."

"Hmmm, that would have been so disgusting without airtight tankers." Efemena covered her nose like she could smell the stench.

"Yeah, that task was not an honourable profession. Workers usually wore masks and big cloaks so no one could identify them. Our parents pleaded we were not to laugh or mock them packing excrement as a means of livelihood. But we could not help it. There was a day two of my friends and I laughed at him. Next morning, we found out he, Ebelebe's husband, was the one who dumped all the faeces he had gathered around the neighbourhood at our verandas. Stench was a killer!" They laughed uncontrollably.

"We are yet to relax, and these insects have begun feasting on us." Efemena peered at her mother and saw she was not perturbed by the tiny insects. "Hmm, Izu, it seems you are friends with these creatures, you are so at ease. Don't they bite you?"

Enatomare smiled. "Of course they do, but my skin is used to them. Their kisses recognize my toughness. Mena, we have seen worse. You see, when we were young girls, lice dealt with us seriously. It messed us up really bad. For those that were malnourished, they died after losing too much blood as they were being suckled round the clock."

"Is it same lice found on dogs?" Her eyes widened.

"Exactly, Mena. Lice inhabited and reproduced in our hairs. Boys were a bit spared, but girls were unlucky because it was improper for us to cut our hair. We grew our hair to make competitive styles for Christmas and New Year celebrations. Hmmm, I remember in those days; we had to make a choice between Christmas and school wears."

"Aha, why, why was that?" Efemena was surprised.

"Igho, money was insufficient. Your parents would ask whether to buy Christmas cloth or school uniforms. You either chose to wear fine dresses for the celebration, or a new uniform, from beginning till the end of a session."

"That is serious. I bet you chose clothes, because you are a fashion dame. Of course a beautiful dress was needed to compliment your hairdo." Enatomare patted her curls to feel if its elegance was still intact. It was glowing even though she was yet to bathe and brush it with activator gel.

"Are you talking about me? You should have known Ediri. She was the most beautiful and choicest maiden amongst all. Every young man vied for her hand. She rejected one suitor or the other with reasons such as: short, ugly, disabled; mere shortcomings. In those days, if we had to write a message that was longer than an A4 paper, we recorded the words in cassette instead, hid it in solid food items and sent abroad to suitors and admirers."

"That was DHL back then," Efemena smiled.

"Exactly. She wanted a man as perfect as cut diamond and one day, a handsome man came from the city. Ediri later found out she married a man with deformities. His left ear was gone, right was scarred and he walked with clutches, a leg lost at war!"

"Hey! Oh my goodness!" Efemena tapped her feet on the ground.

"A cousin came to marry her in the husband's stead."

"That's pure deceit. I hope she left the marriage."

"Mena, she could not have ever done that. It was how ugly men married wives in those days. No girl agreeably goes into union with them. It was irreversible then. The laws stated that a married woman's home was with her husband no matter what, unless she was inherited as a widow."

"The tradition is no better than those lice then," Efemena replied, irritated.

"Yes, lice, that situation created a bond amongst siblings.Old men who rarely cut their beards, would invite children to their houses to pick fat lice from their head. Once in a while our parents got us powder. My father would use a pump to puff lice powder into our hair at night. We covered our noses because that chemical was powerful. The sight of lice falling off made me shiver, goose pimples would rise and plaster my skin for hours. Thereafter, Mama would severely tie an headgear on our heads. Lord, Mena! Those creepy things would dance disco, the head would itch so much one was tempted to remove the headgear but that would be a waste of resource, time and above all, the relief we would derive." Efemena shivered as goose bumps became visible on her arms.

"That must have been harsh, it is amazing how you survived those environmental menaces." Efemena shook her head.

"There was no season for it, every day it was pain but we were used to it. When I married your father, some of them followed me to the city." She smiled, but it disappeared in an instant.

"Gross. Wow!"

"I was embarrassed at a point that I had to make myself comfortable on the floor, rather than our matrimonial bed."

"Did Oso complain?"

"No, he never did, it was just a personal resolve on my part, Mena. In fact, your father bought me lots of hair relaxers. I consistently relaxed my hair until they faded out. He was such a kind and loving man."

Efemena smiled at the tone of adoration in her mother's voice. She knew Izu loved her husband so much. Cooking meals every day for him meant a refreshment of their union. No matter how late, Aruegodore never ate a meal that had stayed over twenty-four hours at home. Her countenance became gloomy as she recalled that her father sought divorce from this awesome woman.

"Izu?" The disturbed tone in her daughter's voice brought Enatomare back from the fantasies of her youth.

"What is it, my child? Omoteme, why do you look so gloomy?"

"Izu, why is Oso acting this way towards you? Goodness knows you could not have done what he is accusing you of. I know that if a wife allows any other man cross her thighs other than her husband, her children fall ill and die one after the other. If she does not confess and get cleansed through traditional rites, her husband will also die. We are hale and hearty therefore his claim is not true. What is happening? Please, you can talk to me." She placed her mother's hand on her bosom.

After thirty-four years of wedlock, Aruegodore questioned Enatomare's commitment to their culturally ordained marriage. She kept these to herself, she did not let her children know how she had lived for years with a man who had zero care for her emotions or loyalty to their vows.

"Hmm. Mena, my daughter, it is all just a charade. Your father had a sweetheart he was supposed to get married to. Unfortunately for him, he had to break the relationship off when he inherited me as a widow. Mena, the lady is widowed now. They readily rekindled their passion. I can't beat their love, Mena. It seems I would fade away when she comes into your father's house."

"No, Izu! Never! That would never happen. Definitely not in this time would father do such a thing. Be positive. My siblings and I will stop this madness. You just have to show us that we are not acting like overgrown fools."

"But they are lovers, they have always been. I should give your father the happiness I have deprived him in the past."

"That is where you got it all wrong, Iz-u-me. He is no longer a boy. He should think and act like a principled man guided with age-long wisdom."

"Mena, you do not understand. Matters of the heart are not easily subdued."

"Please, I do not mean to be disrespectful, but let us end this discussion."

"Mena?"

"Izu."

"As you wish. But promise me, Mena, that you would not relay our discussion to Akpos. Both of you will not approach your father on this matter?" Efemena's silence told Enatomare she would not. Efemena stared into space. She did not hear as her mother left to have her bath. Enatomare scrubbed her body to peel off unforeseen dirt. She jerked one knee to scrub her foot but fell with a thud, a sharp pain shot up her thigh. Enamatore sang sorrowfully from the pain in her heart and thigh:

"Onomine Erhiroghene–whom do I look up to spirit of God?"

"Ah! Eseresharebeluo! Eseresharebeluo!"

"Men are hard to please."

She poured water on her soapy body and removed the wrapper that had served as the door to cover up. As she walked into the house, she looked away from the family's shrine to avert its wrath, if purposely stared at. For Irahun, a woman must not look at its nudity. It was only lenient with those ignorant of the rule.

While in the village, Aruegodore refused to share a bed with her. Efemena's heart shattered when she came in one early morning to discover that her father occupied the bed, while her mother slept on a mat. She was hurt by how their relationship had soured for some time now. On a frightful night, the issue escalated when Aruegodore retrieved a white calabash from their bedside. He held a rifle to her forehead and vowed to shoot her if she did not swear by the pot which had a slain white hen, that no other man had crossed her thighs after their marriage vows. Sleepy Efemena had gone out of her room to fetch water from the clay pot moulded fittingly to the earth and shaded by a tall Udara tree when she heard the gunshot. The trigger echoed like warfare. The cold water could have slushed down Efemena's sapped throat, but shivers raced up her spine when she heard her mother scream. After that day, a thin strand held their union until its fate was decided by the elders.

Human feelings are natural emblements. There is no human on earth that has no emotional entanglements, however, it comes in different shades, being expressed sensitively or insensitively.

Love does not choose who or what it cherishes. It has been said that 'love is blind,' it does not mean that sights are cased in total darkness. However, it signifies how people grope to love and be loved. Human beings with their eyes open, hearts welcoming, soul confronting, cannot stop the power of attraction which lures one to an opposite sex, with almost everything uncommon or unpleasing in their attitudes or appearances.

❧‖ *Two* ‖❧

Away from all the drama in their family, Efemena and Akpos took a drive to Umutu-Umuaja, to feel nature's essence near River Ethiope. The river is one of the deepest inland waterways in Africa; about one hundred and seventy-six kilometers long. The serenity of the environment made them forget the troubles that loomed.

River Ethiope's source is at the foot of a giant silk-cotton tree. It flowed through seven local government areas in Delta State. Its connection to Sapele makes it deep enough to provide harbour for ocean-going vessels.

They enjoyed fishing, canoeing, and swimming. They also ate varieties of sea foods.

"Akpos, what are we to do about Oso and Izu? Brother, their marriage cannot end like this. A woman should not cause rift in our family."

"Yes," he said chewing kpokpo garri. He withdrew a stick of pork wrapped in plantain leaf.

"We must do something fast." Efemena sneezed.

"Mena, the day a mosquito lands on your testicles is the day you will know that there are better ways of resolving issues without violence. We have to tread carefully. There is a place that is rowdy from dawn to dusk, but at night, it is as dead as a graveyard. We should not dance in frenzy at the market square, and forget that when the day is grey, every man carries his basket to his hut."

Akpos removed the straw from the coconut he was drinking, and pushed his sun glasses up his forehead. "This is our parents we are talking about, that woman has no meaning in our lives. Rest, Efemena, everything would be fine, just trust me, okay?"

Efemena nodded though not convinced. She picked at her barbecued catfish, a special she could ravish to the bones any other day.

Efemena felt uneasy. She squished her buttocks on the rock she sat. Akpos looked quizzically at her and burst out laughing when she began to sweat profusely.

"Aha! The magic of palm wine is working on you, Omoteeko. You said you would not use the bush at nature's call with your Oyibo's buttocks eh? You cannot escape this now. Today, we will know whether your forefathers came from Naija, or they fell from heaven!" He looked at his wristwatch and told Efemena they had fifteen minutes' drive to any motel or good eatery where she could use their toilet. The resort's guest house was locked.

"Akpos, we should get going. I feel uncomfortable," Efemena said as she pressed each palm to her buttocks as if they could stop nature's call. "I think I am going to wee in my pants, too, oho! Aw."

"You have not seen anything yet, you go shit for bush today."

"Oh no, brother, let's go, I beg you."

"I'm not moving oh girl, fine baby no pimples, city babe. I thought fine girls like you do not poo." Akpos' wild laughter rustled Efemena's bowels. She comically held her buttocks and ran to the nearest bush.

"Bro, please bring some pawpaw leaves for me," she faintly called after her brother. Akpos laughed till tears watered his eyelashes.

While Efemena was gone, a drama was brewing between two women; a son to one had been accused of stealing groundnut, Akpos watched amusedly.

"You claim there are different snacks for him to eat at will eh? Your son has stolen my food like a little thief, yet you're defending him. Indeed, he cannot get attracted to peanuts because you are the Big Madam Baker, local meat-pie maker. But I ask you, can a dog tell its legs from its hands?"

"Where is the evidence he took your filthy groundnuts?" the mother of the scrawny looking boy asked darting her eyes about. "Where is it you wretched troublesome woman, where is it, Oredia? Can anyone find a single nut on my son?"

This time confidently, she searched her son; turning out his shorts and shirt's pockets. Some people were looking at her with curiosity, snorting, hissing, and murmuring as they awaited truth or lies to be unveiled.

The accuser became worried. She realized particles of groundnut were not on him. He had taken some nuts from the hut she fried peanuts; she had seen him run away.

The dwindling crowd redirected their stares, now intently fixed on her; and those eyes definitely held suspicion. She pondered, chewed her bottom lip.

The boy's mother felt victorious and dragged her son's hand so they could leave.

"Get up from there, let's leave this place before this wretched woman and nosy people would crucify us, my dear. It is their sons and daughters who are thieves not mine." She hissed loudly.

An irritated old lady shouted, "Hey, why are you making such generalizations on people because they have come to witness this drama, and possibly settle any quarrel? What wrong have we done by gathering here, wouldn't you have done the same in such a sensitive issue as this, as a caring mother?"

"I wonder o," some people chorused while the men took their leave before a woman not older than their wives and daughters at home would further insult their manhood, they said aloud. But the women stayed on to see the end of the event.

The old woman spoke up again. "It is not over yet." She said as the little boy's mother made to leave with him. "Somebody get some water, enough of uncalled for accusations and insults, the truth or lie must be established." Before she finished speaking, two women had run off to get water in a cup from the river.

The boy's mother shouted, "God forbid I let my son drink from your witchy cups. This water they have poured cows, goats and chickens blood for sacrifices. Take this rubbish from my son, don't get near him." She pushed them away.

"Here, take this." Akpos gave her a sealed bottled water. He knew the conclusion on seeing the boy fidget. She removed the seal.

"Open your mouth."

His mother had no objection. She poured it into his mouth and asked him to gaggle which he did with hesitation.

"Now pour out the water." He did and along came particles of groundnuts. There was uproar from the thin crowd, the boy admitted his guilt. His mother was ashamed and asked for forgiveness.

Just then, a group of dancers trooped down, heading towards the river. Dance is a core element of Igbe. Adherents believe dancing draws joy from the monotheistic God, and in the beginning, Oghene brought Orhen to the world:

Odie emu ri non he

(It did not start today)

Odie emu ri non he

(It did not start today)

Obo ri kokokri ughe me vwa rhino?

(All of you are gathered here; do you come to watch me dance?)

Orhen me te obo Akare yo!

(My Orhen has spread as far as Benin City!)

Abo out re dje no Igbe vwa ghogho ho

Those of you who ran from Igbe do not rejoice)

The Igbe worshippers sang native Urhobo song in a procession led by a priest. They were garbed in white dresses and white headgears. Older people carried trays on their heads with unripe plantain, fowl and bottled drinks in them.

Akpos did the unthinkable, what Efemena could not believe he would. He pulled off his brown leather jacket, revealing a white round necked polo shirt. He brought a white wrapper and tied it on top of his black jeans.

"Brother, don't tell me you are doing this. Don't tell me you will delve into this act again," Efemena frowned in disapproval.

"What do we have to offer ourselves if not our tradition in its originality, especially the spirituality involved in it. I advise other tribes not to demean their culture. Our values and beliefs should be upheld with pride. When a people's heritage is lost, they become depraved of their peculiar identity. We Africans should not abandon our culture for that of the western world. Mena, I will be back."

He ran to join the procession. The scowl on Efemena's face could melt ice. They stopped worshiping Igbe for long; since their parents embraced Christianity. She knew Akpos still had ties with Igbe religion, but she did not know it was to this extent.

He was fully involved. She watched her brother become eccentric and act insanely. He danced wildly like someone possessed by a mad spirit. She locked the car and followed behind, seething with rage at her brother's participation. An Orhen fell off Akpos's jacket she hung on her shoulders.

Efemena could not resist; she dusted it on her skirt then chewed it with relish. She hurried after them; they were close to the river. She got in line and nudged Akpos with her buttock.

"You planned this all along didn't you? Eh, brother. You knew today is Igbe's annual worship. Why didn't you come on your own, am I your handbag?" Akpos played deaf to her questions as he fervently danced and sang hymns.

"Akpos!" Realizing she had screamed a little loud, Efemena covered her mouth and looked around, but all devotees were engrossed in the procession.

"Efemena Aruegodore, that's your name, an African is who you are, so am I. I hold the gods of my ancestors in reverence and supremacy to Oyibo God. Mena, when man served his ancestors at a personal shrine; he was moral and contented. In his confusion to involve in religious multiplicity, he became exposed and consumed by an insatiable quest to satisfy alien doctrines. He dragged his feet from one temple to another; needing miracles where manna falls from the sky giving way to absurdities and bouts of immoral precedencies. He did obscene things to see food fall from heaven. How will that be possible when he had a shaky faith and split loyalty? Have you ever seen food fall from the sky? Eat Orhen given by our forefathers, be filled with ancestral spirit and blessed growth."

"Akpos!" Efemena shrieked.

"People decide to choose their own god and mode of worship, and also stick to their faith. Man has created various religions in the world, believing one from the other is superior. Why didn't people cling to their one true heritage which they can use to distinguish themselves globally, especially in spiritual ordinance? Look at the chief priest of Igbe shrine, to pay homage give him just kola. But your pastors, they incessantly burrow holes in people's purses." Akpos made a tremendous cycle and danced on. Efemena brooded with each slow step she took.

Igbe religion celebrated an annual feast–Ore Isi for twelve days which takes place every May. Igbe was birthed when Ubiecha Etarakpo graced his eyes upon an apparition of two divine beings who anointed him to preach against immorality and witchcraft. According to the myth, he went to his farm and fell into a trance having eaten native chalk, given to him during an encounter with the divine spirits. Ubiecha became unconventional and acted strangely after he regained consciousness.

A woman, Oniruesi, noticed something mysteriously divine about him, unlike others, who thought he had gone round the bend. He dwelled in her apartment and danced every day, eating Orhen.

His gifted spirituality brought him fame and wealth. People

from around and across Delta, sought his divinations. Ubiecha performed amazing miracles; accurately predicted one's future, healed the sick and identified witches. He built a worship house called 'Ogua' in his compound. From there, ministered to people, his prophesies were in line with truism.

Igbe religion emphasizes purity of mind, body and soul of its members. This is why members are seen wearing white, a symbolism of their pure state. They believe in afterlife. Once a person dies, his soul is reunited with God until a new body is created for the soul to come back to earth. Hence, they believe in reincarnation as is normal in Delta cosmology.

✡ ✡ ✡ ✡ ✡

On their arrival to the village, Efemena heard from their little cousins that Enatomare had been summoned by the elders. Both of them went to their rooms, children were not allowed in the meeting.

She paid her respect when she was called to speak. "My elders, degwo," Enatomare curtsied to the elders, and they jointly responded "Vrendo."

She bent her head and stared at her folded hands which she placed on her thighs. "My husband, before the entire clan has accused me of being an unfaithful wife. My people, today all my children are alive. He says I have cheated on him on countless occasions yet, none of our three children have fallen ill or died. I have nothing to confess, I am innocent of these accusations. If any of you are in doubt of my honour and virtue; though my Christian faith forbids it, I shall perform rites to prove my innocence. I cannot risk the life of my children for the pleasures of another man. May earth curse me to be still if I have ever lusted after another man apart from my husband who paid my dowry, provided me provisions and security and sponsored my education." The elders nodded at her words.

"You may sit down, our wife," the Okpako of the clan said

to Enatomare.

"Degwo," she greeted him and took her seat close to her husband who averted his face when tears began to slide down her eyes.

"My fellow elders, without wasting our time, I will go straight to the point. It is great injustice for Aruegodore to accuse his wife of infidelity and it is an insult to the eldres for him to gather us in this petty frame-up." Enatomare looked at him with shock in her eyes. She blinked her eyelids and shut them again to pray.

"Omamerhi!" Aruegodore called in a surprised tone.

"Do not interrupt me, Aruegodore."

"I would not take this form of slander to my person, Omamerhi."

"Let me finish."

"Omamerhi!"

"I said keep quiet! Shut up I say, Aruegodore! You speak of integrity while you stoop this low to wreck the upright virtues of this woman. I am disappointed in you. I never for once considered that with your status and upbringing, you would put up this charade of a ditched spouse whereas the honeypot of bees is feasting on your senses so much that you lack nobility. What height of indecency you spew as if the word courtesy or honesty has no meaning to you." Omamerhi was furious, while Aruegodore succumbed to moral defeat. He had confided in him, but obviously, his uncle did not buy it.

"Osharena, what Omamerhi has said, does it hold any truth?' an elder asked. Aruegodore bowed his head into his sweaty palms.

"Osharena, I ask you again. Is it true that you have accused your wife falsely because of the sweetness of another woman's thighs?" He did not say a word.

"Aruegodore, the breast of a man should be as firm as his ego. You have got no principle."

"Elder," Aruegodore said.

"Speak the truth. Our ears await your own side of this accusation. Be quick, our grey hairs do not deserve this dance of shame." He stamped his walking stick, and some of the tiles cracked.

"Hey!" one of the elders exclaimed.

"Omamerhi has said the complete truth." Aruegodore burrowed his head deeper in his palms as shame screamed from his admittance.

An elder walked out and returned with a white male goat. "Enatomare?"

"Elder." She dabbed her eyes, stood up and curtsied. The elder placed the rope holding the goat in her hand.

"Our wife, this is for you. The elders celebrate you as a virtuous woman. We present this goat to you. Please, do not take your husband, our kinsman's deed to heart. If you can, increase the shower of your love. Omoteme, rain it torrentially on him."

"Degwo," she replied as she accepted the goat and tied the rope around her right wrist. The elders filed out, each patting Enatomare as they exited.

The Ovwuvwe festival was for the traditional warlords of Umiaghwa, Abraka kingdom who returned from Uyo Forest to the ancestral shrine of Ovwuvwe dancing with people at Ughele-Otorho Abraka. The celebration brought Abraka people together to fratenize, assess their development growth and celebrate their traditional institution. The festival attracted lots of visitors and tourists from various parts of the state. It was celebrated yearly to appease the gods of the land and pray for peace in the community. Efemena had forgotten about the Ovwuvwe festival. She and Akpos had come to the town to print her call-up letter for national youth service.

The festival committee chairman had in a press conference

assured the public that the festival and coronation anniversary celebration would not affect the public's interest. Security agencies would be dispersed to arrest any miscreant found breaching the law.

There was restriction of movement on that day as a result of the festival. After they safely drove to their younger sister's off-campus hostel, Akpos and Efemena stayed in the two-bedroom apartment Akpevwe shared with a course mate. It was Akpevwe that updated Efemena that she could have printed the letter in any cyber café around the village. She collected money to print the letter in the cyberspace a student operated in her compound. Akpevwe came back and handed the letter to Efemena who was sitting outside with Akpos and some of the neighbours in the hostel.

Efemena opened the letter to check for her state of deployment. She screamed and jumped when she saw Abia State. Akpos and the other neighbours congratulated her.

"You are lucky you were not posted to the North. I cried my eyes out when I was posted to the North-east," a female occupant said.

Her husband came up behind her. "And who says the East is better than the North, Madam?"

"I have not said so, dear," she replied her husband.

"You better don't start. Just wish her well. I do not know why you are yet to win an award as the most controversial man in Abraka."

The male occupant jeered on. "Corps members detest Abia eh. My friend said that every *corper* prayed never to be posted to Nawg land. He said they eat human flesh. My friend said he was fortunate to have left that land in peace. They even sell it at restaurants."

Efemena became defensive as she replied the man. "Can you tell me where he served in Nawg? Tell me his PPA; was it a school or a ministry? Give me as much details as you can. I want to do some investigations on your false claims. Just imagine such balderdash. I go there for business like I am trotting my bedroom to parlour and I have never witnessed such nonsense."

Akpos supported Efemena. "I served in Nawg and that was where I married my wife. I did my national youth service there some years ago when it was not even developed and never for once did I hear or see a joint where human parts were being served as bush meat. If you are sure of your claims, why don't you give the address of the restaurant or a description? I will find out the truth in less than twenty-four hours. How can you stay within these walls and taint the image of an industrious community? Stop this falsehood. Nawg people do not eat humans. You are so blind despite been born in the twenty-first century." Akpos shook his head and hissed.

"Put your things in the car Mena and let us get out of here. It is getting late, Izu must be worried. Father has been calling." He looked at his wristwatch.

"Who are those blacklisting Nawg people?" A male student came out angrily from his apartment. "I am disappointed in you, Mr Man, why spread such wicked tales? This rubbish has got to stop. You do not have to fuel this stereotypical trash. I am a Nawg man and I have never tasted human flesh in my life. I don't even know what it smells or tastes like. Can you swear there is anybody's flesh that has ever been eaten in that land? Didn't your friend return from service whole? Is this how non-indigenes repay us for been accommodating? I am so disappointed in you."

"Please, my neighbour, do not mind my husband, you know how he is. I apologize on his behalf. Honey, please apologize," the female occupant pleaded.

"I am sorry. I admit my mistake, I am so sorry." Her husband moved close to the student to pat his shoulder, but the enraged man roughly shoved his hands off.

"Please, take your filthy hands off me. What evidence do you have that Nawgs eat human flesh? At least we have seen your fellow tribesman arrested for trading human flesh."

The student attacked further. "God will punish you if you do not provide tangible evidence of what you have just said about Nawg. Rubbish. Except you provide a lead, vampires will rule your miserable life. That's a curse for your generation. How dare you base your finding on mere assumptions; slandering an entire clan in your foolishness, eh you idiot?" the student fumed.

"He is just very upset, but he will get over it. We know him to be a nice young man," Akpevwe assured Akpos.

"Great" Akpos said, and gave her a thumb up.

"Yeah, he will get over it. He is a peaceful fellow. This is my husband's fault, he would apologize when he comes back." Her husband affirmed her words with nods.

Exotic and accelerating cultural display took place along the old Agbor-Sapele road close to the small market, near Site Two as Akpos drove past. Machetes were used by the dancers to cut one another without it penetrating. Those on bikes scraped their cutlasses on the tarred road birthing fiery sparks and grating sounds; while others carried very dried sacrificial meat for the gods. The chief priest poured fuel on himself and lit a matchstick and to the amazement of everyone, there was no fire. It was indeed a display of the rich cultural heritage of the Urhobo people of Abraka kingdom.

Movements were stopped from two o'clock on that day. Later, students at the Site One area of the university alleged that they were chased and molested. Several hostels were attacked and many students who lived off-campus got robbed of valuable possessions while some girls were sexually harassed. There were reports that students who mingled with the crowd, received various degrees of injuries from machete cuts and were treated at the General Hospital.

As Akpos tried to insert a disc into the stereo, Efemena shouted, "Akpos, watch out!"

He looked ahead and saw some cows that just ran out the road. He swerved the steering with one hand to divert from the road but the gear was stiff in his shaky hands.

"Brother, pull over, pull over."

"Mena, fasten your seat belt."

She scrambled for the rope and fastened it with her eyes fixed on the huge animals that were advancing towards motorists. The herdsmen were nowhere in sight. Akpos mustered strength and courage to put the gear in reverse. He sped backwards as Efemena shouted. A driver, not seeing ahead, overtook Akpos and crashed into one of the cows.

"Oghene!" Akpos exclaimed at the degree of damage.

"Oh my God! Oh my God!" Efemena unstrapped and unlocked the car door after Akpos had parked the car at a safe distance from the cows.

"Wait here, Efemena."

"But, Brother?"

"Sit here." He patted her on the shoulder and came down from the car. He reached the spot and a mighty cow lay lifeless. It was a hard hit. The car bonnet of what used to be a Lexus Jeep was compressed beyond recognition. The driver was badly hurt and had lost consciousness. The road safety corps was alerted and they got to the scene within five minutes.

"Is everyone alright?" the superior asked. He was taken aback when he saw the bloodied car owner. "Oh Lord, my goodness. Officer, get the ambulance, quick. There is an emergency. Go quick."

"Eku General Hospital? There has been an accident. There is an emergency, some miles from Eku junction. Hurry. Thanks." He ended the call. "They are on their way, Sir."

"Get him out" They brought out the tall burly man slowly. "Get the oxygen pack."

"Akpos, is he alright?" Efemena asked from behind him.

He darted his head right and left and turned back. "Efemena, I told you stay in the car."

"Our cow is dead, walai you must pay for this fa," the herdsman said arriving at the scene.

36

"Is this cow yours?" an official asked.

"Yes. It is for me and my brothers." He pointed at two teenagers that held riffles on their shoulders.

"A human being is in critical condition and all you can think of is your damned cow? He shook his head. "You guys are cynical. Leave animals and let us speak of life. Damn it!" Akpos said, infuriated.

The youths in the area trouped out and danced around the cow. After chanting some comrade songs, they lifted the cow, about nine of them, their shouldres and biceps bulging, to the nearest shade. They seized the carcass of the cow and warned the herdsmen that if anything happened to their youth leader; they would kill their cows and send them out of town.

Oxygen was passed to the victim. He was unconscious and was driven in the road safety's patrol van.

"Akpos, did you see that? We could have died. We could have been the victim. Either of us could be lying half-dead like that man."

"Let us praise Oghene, his saving grace kept us alive. That is why this grazing bill should not be passed; else all hell would break loose across the country."

"Oh my God!" Efemena said still in shock. These cattle had become a menace on highways, virtually all roads. Efemena made a sign of the cross, thankful to God to be alive. She was going for the NYSC orientation in some days.

Three

After a tedious journey down from the West to the East, Efemena finally arrived at Umuahia and boarded a bus with other prospective corps members at the park. They travelled to Bende, where the camp was situated.

As Efemena walked through the gates, she saw different officers in uniforms. She was given directions to the police post for checking-in. The female officer rummaged through her bags for any provision defying the NYSC's list. The officer found nothing to rebuff except a thick belt Efemena had bought from an itinerant trader through the window of a bus. It was a breach of the provision law, therefore the lady seized it.

Thereafter, she was asked to write her name in a long register and was given a paper that bore some digits. She was shown the way to the female hostel and asked to go to the storeroom. She extended the paper to the attendant who allowed her to select a mattress. Efemena unveiled the taekwondo and karate skills she learnt from watching movies in order to get a nice foam. It paid off and she got a neat mattress for her efforts.

She moved to the hostel; Efemena chose the C block because it looked less crowded, but she was shocked to see it packed like a tin of tuna fish. She was surprised that majority had come in that same day as herself, much earlier than she presumed; to get fair accommodations, bunk space, good mattress and to escape the hurdles during rush hour.

Luckily for her, she found a superb space at the far end of

the hall. She slid her buckets and bags under the bunk. She quickly brought out her bedspread, blanket, and pillow to lay her bed. She scarcely fixed the mosquito net with thought of enduring it for one night because she was exhausted. Efemena heaved a loud sigh of relief and heard the angry grumble in her stomach, that she has not had dinner. The only meal she had eaten was pounded yam with okro soup at an eatery along the way.

Efemena brought out two plantain chips stashed in her handbag and shook her water flask. "Oh great! This is just great! My water flask is empty. I have to beg on my first day in a new environment."

She asked a corps member directly opposite her for water and the plump lady said she had not a drop to offer. Efemena asked around but nobody had a drop of clean water to quench her thirst.

"So this is how I will sleep in this terrible state," Efemena murmured and almost bumped her head on a top bunk as she made her way through the narrow path, back to her row.

The next day was filled with so many activities. Efemena had all the necessary credentials required by NYSC for the screening exercise; her original school result, from high school to tertiary, NYSC call-up letter and red background passport photographs. She was cleared by the officials who verified her documents with the use of ultraviolet mercury light verification system; they took another photo of her regardless of Efemena's personal copies for the computerized registration. She queued to get a laminated paper with four figures encrypted on it, as well as a meal ticket. She used the number on the card to locate her platoon. She gave her card to the platoon officer who asked her to fill the blank spaces of some forms with vital information and personal details. Some chairs were arranged at the unit, but they were mostly occupied by people's bags. In the absence of a decent seat, Efemena made one by placing her shawl on the floor. Efemena sat leisurely on her improvised chair as she filled in her details carefully to avoid mistakes. Afterwards, the platoon officer shared the NYSC kits serially as they had put down their names on a piece of paper. The kits consisted of a khaki trouser and a matching jacket, an NYSC crested vest, two white round-neck tops, two white shorts, two pairs of white stockings with a mix of green color, a jungle boot with shades of oranges and black, a pair of white shoes with NYSC inscription on it, a cap, a soft green belt, booklets comprising of NYSC Bye Laws and Orientation/Service Guide Handbook of Language Study for Corps Members.

It was stated in the handbook that a prospective corps member would only be mobilized if he was under the age of thirty. But Efemena could see older men and women as corps members. After her registration, she dashed off to her hostel happy to transform into the white uniform. Efemena quickly had her bath, making it the second time she would shower to make up for not bathing last night. She was amazed she had no dreaded mosquito bite since she did not fix the mosquito net last night. It was at the registration hall that Efemena learned that the whole vicinity had been fumigated. She noticed that the grasses had also been mowed. Efemena hurriedly wore a short, a top, socks, cap, and the identification card hung loosely around her neck. She also had a waist pouch on. This was the required uniform for corps members.

The Mammy market bubbled with corps members still in mufti and *otondo* uniforms like Efemena's. The mammy market comprised of small makeshift stalls constructed for each trader.

There were displays of different goods and services such as restaurants, barbing and hair-dressing salons, medicine and provision stores, game house, boutique, photographer stands, a bookshop, barbecue stand, bar corner and other attractions. Efemena raced to a commercial centre for charging electrical appliances and flashlights. Phones of different brands and sizes had serial numbers plastered on them for easy identification by their owners. Efemena's battery level was low. She removed the battery and gave the operator fifty naira (₦50) to charge it. She obtained a plastic card, which bore a number plastered on it.

She sauntered into a restaurant that sold noodles and egg, bread and tea and ordered noodles and egg. She ate excitedly as she was happy to experience what she had heard from past corps members who oftentimes described the camp as Sodom and Gomorrah due to the many activities that happened there. "My dear, the days in camp are not for saints. I can already hear tales of pants and boxers escapades and see condoms lithering the orientation ground in the morning," Efemena excitedly spoke to Fola over the phone as she waited for her meal.

As the days went by, it dawned on Efemena that the camp life was restrictive. Weekdays were for serious activities while on Sundays, most Christians aligned themselves to the houses of worship registered on camp – the Nigerian Christian Corpers Fellowship and the Nigerian Association of Catholic Corpers. The Muslims had a makeshift mosque for prayers on Fridays.

It was the period of fast and Muslims were allowed to go for ablution and prayers. They were served their meals earlier, before and after the break of fast. This made some Christians pretend to be Muslims. Efemena was amused at how the penchant for food could make some people deny their religion.

The sound of the beagle signalled one activity or the other. It woke corps members up by four-thirty in the morning. They moved to the parade ground. At the parade ground, corps members sang the national and NYSC anthems, the OBS crew gave the camp news while the camp officials gave all other formal addresses and announcements. Thereafter, physical exercise and drills were conducted by the platoon team officer and army officers. Parade training ultimately started with the indomitable Nigerian Army giving orders. Sanitation followed, supervised by NYSC officials who apprehended defaulters hiding in hostels and the mammy market in order to avoid the mandated duty. The beagle called for orientation lectures and meals. It sounded at lunch time, siesta, evening parade, dinner and finally light out.

Efemena joined the orientation broadcasting service. She auditioned and was given the role of chief duty continuity announcer. She and some other corps members woke up before two in the morning to bathe and dress. At the sound of the Beagle, at four-thirty, they walked to the parade ground with ease. If one was not on the parade ground, the soldiers would punish the defaulters by making them do frog jump or chant, "If you are not on the parade ground, you are wrong. If you are late and still walking, you are so wrong, so double up!"

At the swearing-in-ceremony, prospective corps members were dressed in their complete uniform. They were like paramilitary of a million battalion. Many eminent individuals graced the occasion – the governor of the state was also present with some of his appointees and dignitaries and their elaborate entourage.

After camp, some corps members disappeared. They paid some officials money and were seen at the end of the service year or never again, but got their discharge certificates.

Efemena and other corps members that had been posted to the same local government left the camp for their place of primary assignment. She submitted her posting letter and got accepted. Efemena reported at her local government office before travelling to Lagos. She submitted her letter for a few weeks, vacation addressed to the State Coordinator, through the Zonal Inspector to prepare for resumption. She needed to spend time with her family before settling in the East for the long year. Efemena decided Akpos' house would be her first stop as she boarded a bus to Lagos.

❧| *Four* |❧

Efemena was getting cold despite wearing an overall coat on top of a thick cardigan. It was drizzling; the rain had subsided but it had caused a flood resulting in a serious traffic jam. The straight road divided consciously by motorists into two lanes was at a halt. A big trailer had run out of fuel while turning into the street from the major road and suspended movements. Drivers bound to take the highway had no option than to turn off their engines as their tires struggled in the pool of water. Some had their feet swimming in water that had seeped into the car. Those with sophisticated foot wears pulled them off, while school children hoisted their legs on the car seats or were carried in the arms of their parents and guardians.

The impatient Lagos passengers hopped on available commercial bikes whose riders could maneuvre their ways between car trunks, doors, bonnets and move in any free path that could connect them to the major road, not to be deterred from the day's business. Some drivers, envious of their fortune, screamed and rained curses on them not to scratch or splash water on their vehicles. A hefty man in a rickety Prado jeep consistently blared his horn consciously as though it would ease the traffic but he was causing more distraction. Efemena was getting weary because she had to trek in the water; its force hindered her from making fast strides. She tried to stay off the gutter because falling into it would crown the shitty day. Everywhere was messed up, yellowish water streamed in thin lines and flowed into the gutter, obviously, fecal matter that had been washed out from burst sewers. In Efemena's effort to dodge an *Okada* man, she veered off the road and bumped into a *Danfo* bus.

"Haba, this is madness! Do you want to kill somebody?" she called out to the bike man who did not care if he had injured anyone.

She took time to rest on the bonnet of a vehicle that steamed warmth. Efemena sought some kind of heat from its engine that was still revving. The driver from an exchange between him and his conductor said that if he put off the engine, they and some passengers would have to push the vehicle for it to start again. His bus had just joined other endless cars. As Efemena heaved her body on the bonnet, she heard a sound like a zipper being drastically undone; and a flash of cold hit her nape. She panicked and tried to hold on to the split fur garment. She glanced at her shoulder and saw the fresh cut.

She almost tripped over some wares as a wavering tricycle forced her to step on the pedestrian walk for safety. The saleswoman used her body to prevent her goods from falling on the muddy ground. She became furious and with voice seethed in anger began cursing Efemena.

"What is this nonsense, you stupid woman?"

"Hey! I beg you do not shout at me! I am sorry, okay?" She held her right hand up.

"You are a very clumsy human being, you almost damaged my goods."

"Haba, Madam, but I said you should not vex, it has not gotten to the stage you rain all these insults on me."

"Is it your apologies that would have saved my goods?"

"But they did not fall off and even if they had, I would have definitely paid for them."

"Come on, get away. That decrepit money you have been paid by your customers. I would not bring curse on my business."

Some passers-by laughed at the woman's utterance and

gave Efemena suspecting looks with the way she was dressed. She walked away feeling a bit embarrassed, but stopped to apologize one more time.

"Truly, I am sorry, Ma, do have great sales today, good day."

Another man came down from his bike and cursed the driver. *"Na your children you go go kill for house, thunder fire you and that your useless keke."* He nearly fell from his bike as he stretched his hand to hit the roof.

✲ ✲ ✲ ✲ ✲

An hour later, Efemena walked into her brother's living room; her clothes had dried.

"Degwo, Brother, Magare?" she curtsied and took a seat facing Akpos.

"Vrendo? my dear, I am very fine, thank you. As you can see, I am as good as any newly married man."

"Oh sure. I can see that, and our wife?"

"She is doing fine. Isn't my wife taking good care of me?" He stretched his arms to show off. *"We full ground."*

"Hmmm, you need not tell me more, I am convinced. You are looking nice, Brother." She winked at him, and just then there was power outage. They made displeased sounds. Efemena was surprised to see Akpos getting up. "May I ask, Brother, where are you heading to?" she asked him curiously.

"Do I need permission to move about in my own house again, Madam? Anyway, I am going to put on the generator."

"My big brother of life! Hmmm, what has changed? I am sure if Mother had been sitting with us when this happened, you would not have moved. Even when we pleaded that you should put on the generator to complete a movie, you insisted that the scarcity of fuel will not permit you. But now you readily put it on without anyone asking, no pressure whatsoever to do so and knowing fuel has become gold of late."

"Those are your opinions and they are free."

"Hmm. Is that all you will say?"

"Do you think I will give you any more details? Please excuse me. I cannot subject my wife to heat, she is having a well-deserved rest." He smiled like a boy given candy. "So, whatever, Madam, I'm off; my baby might be getting distressed over the lack of nice air any moment from now."

"Yes, boss, my opinion does not count in this matter for sure." Efemena gave him a military salute.

"Ehen, thank goodness you know, so please excuse me." He bowed mockingly and made to leave.

Efemena was about to cross her legs as Akpos was leaving. "Hey, Mena, do not sit that way in my living room I beg you. Aha! I have told you countless times to stop dressing like this. It is not responsible, and society will tag you an immoral lady. This gown is too revealing for goodness sake. Couldn't you have worn something better?"

"Like the wrapper for village meeting? Brother Akpos, please save me these sermons. Society can say whatever they like, they do not know a thing about me, and I do not care what they think. They neither pay my bills nor stock my wardrobe."

"My dear sister, society will always care. It is an interference you have no control over, so you should begin to care, and act with it because they will always talk, you hear!"

"Whatever. Please go and turn the generator on for your pretty wife, *Oga* married man."

"Oh yes I will and you should begin to think that no responsible man is likely to marry a woman like you. Take these words from a friend, a man and a brother, Mena."

"I have heard you. Go now please."

"I have told you, and will keep telling you the truth, dear. If you decide to use those wrappers to sew gowns, skirts, trousers and what have you; I will love your outfit."

"Hmm, when did you become a fashion designer, Bro?"

"Let me finish, Mena. Do you know you can actually sew grand styles with ankara, George and that frilly material? Hmm, what do you call it again?" He thought for some seconds. "Yeah. Chiffon, that is it and you can make fabulous designs out of them. Mena, you know these stuff, apply them to business and to your personal wardrobe. And make them reach your knees at least!" He scoffed as she tugged at the gown.

"I would be the happiest man if you can do that. I know you are a good woman in and out. Do not give people room to think otherwise about you."

"Thanks, my darling Brother. I have heard; just watch me do my thing."

Her eyes glowed at the different business prospects that were flooding her mind. "I could create designers that would trend. Now go, Brother. I also need that generator so that the fan can cool my head." Efemena waved Akpos off with a snort. When he had gone, the scene at the market where the saleswoman heaped derogatory statements about her played in her head. Efemena clapped her hands in awe of her brother's ideas and smiled fondly.

She brought out a fashion magazine from her handbag. It had different designs and outfits for celebrities and lovers of fashion. Colours were the trend in fashion with the females steering the wheels, vying with passion to get the best colour combinations. The male folks did not exempt themselves as they stayed up-to-date with classic colours. Men were elegantly dressed in traditional suit with and without a tie, with the pocket-square folded or arranged neatly in the breast pocket. Even with the African society being filled with western styles of dressing, traditional outfits are not overlooked. The designs cannot phase out because they give a unique identity. The African wardrobe is one of inestimable value to its people. A Nigerian may put on clothes sewn from ankara, George, lace, and wear to their places of work on Fridays. This is not the usual tying of wrappers, but gown attires and scarfs to match; with the wearing of glasses, to match with any colour of the cloth. As Efemena admired the contents of the magazine, her attention was jerked from the paper she was reading when screams filtered into the apartment. She dashed out when she heard Akpos calling for the gateman not to bring a machete.

"Akpos, what's it Brother?"

"Mena, stay back!" She scampered when she saw a mighty python. She almost fainted but for the gateman who held her from falling.

A woman rolled on the floor, crying, and begging that the snake should not be harmed. "Please, you people should not touch it; if you hurt him then I am dead. Please, my good neighbours let it be, it has come to greet me."

"Mama Onome, what are you saying? How did this big snake find its way into the city, a busy residential area as this and a very neat compound?" a neighbour asked.

"You can see it is humble. Please, you people should not kill it for me, please. It means no harm."

"You people should listen to her," Akpos implored the men who stood at different angles wielding various weapons.

"This is my god oh; it has come to bless me and my family," Mama Onome cried while neighbours looked at each other in confusion.

"Yeah, she is right. They actually worship it. This thing is real and not superstitious, my fine gentlemen. They can sleep on the same bed with it, and these snakes can serve as pillows and cushion for them. Listen, it is a taboo to kill it. Calm down and drop your weapons please, this fright can kill Mama Onome," Akpos said.

"You must be joking, Akpos," Olamide said.

"I speak the truth. They are sacred to them. Do you know that they are buried like human beings? If this particular one dies today; it would be buried six feet deep. So, kill it. I hope your annual salary can bear the cost."

"God forbid I bury a snake!" Olamide shouted.

"Akpos continued. I am sure Mama Onome and her husband can accommodate it since they are from the same village; it can sleep in their home today, and have unrestricted access to any part of their home. If it is seen coiled up somewhere, just leave it to relax until it goes away."

"This is incredible!" another neighbour said.

"It does not get mad. But do not curse or chase it away, like you guys are about to do. My people, we should not be doing that. If you had gone to her village, be assured of total safety and protection, they do not without cause harm visitors," Akpos tried to douse the situation.

"Akpos, God bless you," Mama Onome said.

Akpos continued. "Now that the python is here, it would be entertained by Mama Onome as an August visitor, in which case, she has to treat it like a royalty."

"You are right, Brother. I remember when an oil company employed me and some other people to go and drill a land. We were welcomed by a big boar. It was so huge eh. It circled us about seven times and made its way into the bush. Truly this snake also, it must not be caught, cursed or chased about. The indigenes would not take it kindly, if you kill any of the snakes knowingly or in ignorance, be prepared for the consequences!"

"Eh!" Olamide said.

"Listen, the whole community will be involved. I heard from a friend back there, an indigene. He said at one time, an *Oyibo* man tried to charm snakes at a festival. Being a magician, he thought his crew would succeed. One of the snakes was deposited in the boot; initially the car would not bulge but when it moved, it would not go beyond the outskirt of town. They were rooted to a spot until they were caught."

Olamide placed his hands on his head. "This snake is so big, damn!"

"Come, we should stop acting non-African. Every one of us here has one animal as a totem in our villages if I am not mistaken and I am not because it is true. Mama Onome, please give your guest due hospitality. Most of you here are acting like you do not have such in your various villages," Akpos said.

Mama Onome bowed to the python. She ecstatically called her children to bring food and drinks for offering. After the snake departed, they went into their various apartments, chatting about animals worshipped in different villages.

Five

The next day, Efemena was responsibly dressed. She wore a pencil trouser, and a peplum top sewed with *George* material and a pair of sandals. Many people were on queue at the ATM gallery. Efemena received a call when it was her turn so she allowed someone behind her to use her slot. As soon as she was through with the call, she joined the not so long queue. When it was her turn, she tried her card but the ATM ejected it. She gave up after trying for a while and left the bank. As Efemena walked towards the bus stop, a man called her. "Hi, you remember me?"

"Hi! Yeah, I remember you, you took my slot."

"Yeah, you allowed me to."

"I did, you are right." They laughed.

He extended his hand. "I am Adeniji."

"Pleased to meet you, I am Efemena."

"The pleasure is all mine, pretty Efemena."

"I have to be on my way; do have a splendid day."

"Oh, it seems you are in a hurry?"

"Is it that obvious? Anyway, I am and I have to run."

"I would like us to hang out."

"I cannot. I have to go somewhere else, where I can find an ATM outlet because I could not complete my transaction."

"It must be the BVN registration."

"No I do not think so, I have registered."

"Have you linked it with your other accounts?"

"Linked?"

"Yeah link; it seems you have not. You are not even aware of that procedure."

"True, I didn't know of such process." She twirled the card in her hand.

"Then I will advise you head straight to the bank instead of trying another ATM, it will be the same, and you cannot make any transaction until you have linked all your accounts in any bank with your BVN."

Efemena looked at her wristwatch. "Whoops! I hope I do not encounter delay because registering for the BVN initially was like hell. Thanks so much, you have been of great help to me. Thank you." She clasped her hands together in gratitude.

"Thank you for your time too, pretty, you are welcome."

Efemena smiled and turned to go but he stopped her. "Please excuse me, Efemena." He brought out a complimentary card from his wallet.

"Here is my card. We can still have lunch some other time, please."

Efemena accepted the card with a smile and gave him her card as well. "That's mine; I will keep a date in mind for that lunch. Thank you, bye." She smiled and waved at him.

He nodded. "I can drive you to your nearest bank if you would let me."

"That is enough, Adeniji, I do not want to take any more of your time."

"It is no sweat, I will do it wholeheartedly."

"I insist on my 'no' answer, Sir, bye for now."

Adeniji raised his hands above his shoulders. "Hands up, Ma'am, I give up. I look forward to the date with you some other time though."

"Okay, bye."

"Bye, bye."

Akpos drove into the street and saw Efemena trekking. He pressed the car's horn and she looked back and in a rush, got into the passenger's seat, heaving as she settled.

"Brother, Degwo. Thank goodness you came my way just now, I would have fainted from walking. I am so exhausted. How was your day?"

"My day was great, and yours? You look tired. What have you been up to?"

"BVN."

"BVN?" he asked, and made another turn.

"Yes, I went to link it to my account; I could not use my debit card. But, Bro, I found it hard to breathe in the banking hall. I had to dash out before I collapsed."

"Omote, do you mind telling me what happened to your car? You are supposed to own one if I remember correctly. What happened to it, or better still, what have you done with it? Because I don't know why you walk the whole city on foot lately, *why you dey trek up and down, Efemena, tell me*?"

"I sold it." She playfully pulled her ears.

"You mind telling me why?"

"I had to sell it."

"Yeah I know that, Miss OLX, what you should tell me is for what reason or purpose you had to sell a car I bought for you as a birthday present?"

"I needed to raise funds for my last trip to Dubai, I was low on cash and some of my clients were delaying payments."

"So why didn't you come to me for assistance, Efemena?"

"I didn't want to bother you, Brother; you have been through a lot; your father-in-law's burial and children's tuition. You spent money and you have other responsibilities."

"It is okay, though not alright. Efemena, I just need you to remember one thing."

"Okay, what, Brother?"

"That you are my family, same blood and that you can come to me for anything that is within my capability, remember that, *let it sink into your head, lady*." He poked the side of her cheek.

"I will, Brother, thank you."

"My stubborn sister is acting all big and independent. You will have the keys to my other car, I was about disposing it anyway. You can use it till you can get yourself another car. The driver can join the HR team for now."

Efemena hugged her brother. "Degwo, Bro. God bless you, you are awesome. I don't know what I would have done without you; you are just as kind as Father."

"Yeah, yeah. Who is likely to give your hand out in marriage after Father?"

"You oh!"

"So never forget, I am your daddy also, okay?"

"Yeah, I understand, Sir!"

"Ehen," Akpos nodded his head.

"Bro, that reminds me, I would be travelling to Ibadan this weekend to see our parents."

"Is anything the matter?"

"Nothing actually. I just want to be with them for a while and sell some goods before I leave for my state of deployment."

"That is very thoughtful of you. Extend my regards to them. I will also give you some items for them. You and my wife can go shopping tomorrow."

"And then again; I have to deliver the clothes I got for the Alaafin's Oloris."

"How did you warm your way into the palace? Shuo, Mena, you have gone PLC, see levels. You are now at the top." He was surprised.

"Bro, stop. What is there? You remember my secondary school classmate, Jumoke?"

"Yes of course, that your pretty friend." He grinned.

"Yeah, Brother, the same one you were calling 'my wife, my wife' up and down Ibadan. She is the newest wife of the Oba, and through her influence, I got the contract of supplying artistries. The other wives liked the designs I got for Jumoke, and so, they wanted the same designs from your sister." Efemena clapped her hands and clamped them to her chest in delight.

"Hmmm," Akpos nodded his head. "Now I see why you had to sell your car in order to make the trip to Dubai."

"Exactly, Brother, they wanted some jewelry and foot wears; and Dubai was the business port."

"You are doing excellently well, Omote. More grace, keep the great strides."

"Thanks, Brother, I will." She smiled.

"Efemena, when did you get in? I thought I would be home before you today?" Chinwe hugged Efemena when she arrived home.

"Not long ago, my wife. Welcome. How was service?"

"Fine, my dear. I hope you have eaten, did your brother give you food?"

"What kind of talk is that? Does she not know the way to the kitchen?" He opened his arms to hug his wife and dragged her so she gently sat on his thighs.

"Aunt Chinwe, why didn't you take my brother with you?"

"Does he agree to? The only times he has been to church were the days we got married, thanksgiving and the dedication of your nephews and niece."

"At least I agreed to marry you in the church." He kissed her lips.

Chinwe laughed and said, "You won't change eh, Obim."

"Sweet, leave that thing. Go get me food to eat. Both of you can fast."

Chinwe nudged his arm from her waist and stood up. Akpos smacked her buttocks.

"Super", He winked at his wife who gave him a naughty

look.

"Efemena, let us go to the kitchen. This brother of yours is not serious. Naughty man, see what you are doing in front of my in-law," she snorted.

"And so, are they not my property?" He tried to touch her boobs but Chinwe playfully slapped his hand away.

"Akpos, leave me alone, we can do this in our bedroom."

"Imagine. Didn't your pastor preach to you not to play bad play?"

"Which one is bad play? Is playing with my husband an abomination?" She wriggled her buttocks in his face and made for the kitchen with Efemena.

"Hmmm, I am just glad my nephews and niece are in boarding school. Else you people would have spoilt them."

"It is your brother that has spoilt me oh; this crazy sweet Delta man I married." They all laughed.

After the meal, Efemena cleared the table and washed the dishes. She entered the living room to see Akpos feeding his wife some pineapple slices. She cleared her throat to speak. "You people can make one curse being single." She picked the remote and surfed the channels. She settled for African Magic Yoruba.

Chinwe laughed and gave the tray of fruits to Efemena. "Here, dear."

"Thanks aunty" She took the tray and ate a little.

Efemena saw a telecommunication advertisement and recalled she had a sim card in her bag. She got her bag and brought out the sim. Efemena removed the LOG micro sim from its pack, inserted it in her phone, and switched it on. The settings appeared and she pressed 'accept' for it to be configured. Another came in and said the subscriber should make call as mandated by NCC to avoid disconnection. She tried to dial a number but other messages came in: 'your account has been activated', 'main balance is empty', 'your account has been activated', 'your account has been deactivated'. The last message came in continuously.

"Brother!" she called Akpos' attention.

"Yes, Sister?" He looked up from a newspaper.

"See this sim card I just bought." She brought it to Akpos.

"Let me see." He collected the phone and scrolled through the messages. "When did you buy it?"

"Today."

"What time?"

"In the morning."

Akpos peered at the big wall clock. "It is almost eight. Why didn't you put it on earlier?" He looked at Efemena.

"I felt there was no need since the guy said the prepaid bonus plan will be activated by six o'clock."

"Eh, you said what?" Akpos examined the sim card

"Yes, prepaid. They were having a promo as I passed through Ikotun. It was quite an amazing offer, Akpos. The guys told me that if I bought the sim card at one thousand naira, I would be given five gigabyte, ten thousand naira call credit to any network, and then three months free call credit for LOG to LOG calls."

"Hey!" Akpos was dumbfounded. He shifted so the rear of his buttocks was at the chair's edge.

"So, the guy said it was not an instant thing, it would not work on the spot. New subscribers must be about fifty in number before he sent it to the system to be activated."

"Mena, you have been scammed." He clapped his hands.

"No, no, no, it is real. Their company's bus was there, about two designed LOG official vehicles and the marketers wore customized T-shirts. I was registered with my personal data, snapped and I did biometric signing. The guy said by six in the evening, my sim would be working. He showed me thirty-eight people including myself that had registered and that I should dial *180*7# to get my bonuses."

"You were stupid, Mena." Akpos hissed.

"Aha, Brother, why did you call me stupid?"

"Can't you see the *mumu* thing you fell for? I mean what

telecommunication firm can boast of such bonuses in this crippling economy? The fraudsters got you. And to think you are smarter than this, yet, you were swindled. Chinwe, come listen to super story," he called his wife who appeared from the kitchen.

"What is it, Obim?" She sat at his side. "Efemena, your face looks like you have seen a ghost or something. What happened in my absence?"

"Your in-law was scammed." Akpos narrated the story to Chinwe.

"These people are terrible. Mena, next time, please buy sim cards directly from the company's registered outlets."

Efemena could not believe she had been fooled by some youths. "It is not the one thousand naira that hurts." She shook her legs. "I cannot believe that I, Efemena Aruegodore, was swindled in this *Eko*."

"Anybody can be played, forget that thing. See what *long throat* has caused you." Akpos began laughing. Chinwe could not hide her laughter and she joined her husband. Efemena did not know what to do. She joined the couple to laugh till tears filled her eyes.

Akpos's eyes followed his wife about the room; he removed his reading glasses and placed it carefully in its case.

"Baby?"

"Yes, Obim."

"Come over for a moment please." Chinwe walked towards her husband and sat next to him on the bed. She was ready to place her leg on his thighs, but he stopped her. "Put those legs down, Madam, do not tempt me. I called you for serious talk."

She placed her leg down and sat upright. "Obim, what is wrong? Have I offended you?"

"For several days, I have been seeing Boyoboyo at the

junction. What is happening, Chinwe?"

Chinwe got up and walked to the dresser, her back turned to Akpos. Akpos walked to her and took the hair brush from her. He brushed her long natural hair admirably, mesmerized as the hair settled softly on her shoulder blades

"Last month, you said your church was raising funds to send him to a rehabilitation centre. Why is he still at that dumpsite, smoking?"

Chinwe turned and faced her husband. "Obim, I don't know what to say. I feel embarrassed myself. We ought to have taken him off the street. Pastor Henry is still collecting donations for this cause. He said we need more money."

"But I gave you five hundred thousand (₦500, 000) and I am sure you donated more than that because you crest church matters to your heart. If you ask me, I think you should find out what the delay is about."

"You are right, Honey. After choir practice on Wednesday, I will see the pastor."

"Good. Hmm, you look so lovely." She turned and shoved him away gently.

"Obim, I am not in the mood."

"I know." He caressed her for a while.

"Now you are working me into the mood. See how shamelessly I melt in your arms," she said as she yielded to him. They kissed passionately.

❧ Six ❧

"Sorry, sorry, I am so sorry." She shook her head, solemnly.

"There you said it, which is just it 'sorry'. Sorry is the word, you have finally said it. Apology accepted but, Efemena, this is the end of our relationship. I cannot go on with courtship, or think to spend a lifetime with a woman, who finds it difficult to acknowledge her wrongs and render apologies. I won't last long with someone who cannot own up to her failings, or correct her ways. Goodbye, Mena, I hope the next man you love, you give him this bit of humble submission."

"No, Fola my darling, do not say these words to me, they are breaking me to pieces, you know I cannot take it, please stop." She held up her hand. "Just stop please."

"No, Efemena, I will not, you know I barely hesitate to say the truth. I say it as realistic as they stand where we are concerned. I have waited for you all these years to mend your ways, to treat your baseless ego but no, you would not see from my angle. Even as damn right as they were, you could not conform but would have your way all the goddamn time! Just imagine for how long you have been globetrotting in the name of businesses. You have been around for over a week now and you have not made out time for us to meet, not an attempt, Mena. I am deeply hurt by your carelessness. Maybe you don't love me as much as I do you."

"Fola, please," she said in a quivered tone.

"How do you think our relationship would work?"

"Don't get mad; please be not vexed with me," Efemena pleaded and held the helm of Fola's sweatshirt. He pried her fingers open one by one to take release of his clothes. "I am not vexed; I am just extremely through with this. Goodbye, my sweet love, may our paths cross with success strides in our careers and love life; I love you, all the best."

He looked longingly at her and said 'I love you' one more time before he let himself out of her room, straight out of her life.

With the silent click of the heavy iron door, he walked away. Her heart grieved with so many regrets. But she did not cry, it was all her fault. The Fola she knew would never go back on his words, decisions or actions, she knew better than to go after him. Efemena was heartbroken; she wished her parents were back from their outing so her mother could console her.

Outside, Fola did not look backwards. He exchanged pleasantries with Efemena's parents who had just arrived, like nothing was amiss. But they could feel something was amiss. He bade farewell, got into his car and honked for the gate keeper to open the gate.

"Do you think everything is alright between Fola and our daughter?" Enamatore asked her husband.

"I always knew her pride or something I cannot put my hands on would make holes that cannot be patched in her courtship. I sense our tie with that brilliant young man has been severed. It would be hard if she does not mend her ways. I hope you carried my snuff box from the compartment glove?"

"Yes I did." She showed him the silver box.

"Good, you should have a long talk with your daughter, woman." Enamatore nodded her head like a trader with heavy stock on her head to dispatch.

"Degwo," Efemena greeted her parents as she descended the stairs.

"How are you, Mena? Hope all is well with you and Fola?" Enamatore went straight to the point, seeing her daughter's sad countenance.

"I am fine, Izu." She took her father's walking stick and cap. "Welcome back."

"Mena, you do not look fine. Arue, ask your daughter what the problem is."

"I don't want to talk about this now, please."

"Okay. As you wish." She pulled off her golden headgear.

Efemena collected the headgear as well. "Izu, Mrs Jessa came by. She dropped some files for you; I kept them in the study."

"About time." Aruegodore looked relieved, but Enatomare was sad.

"So I will never see her at the meetings?" She did not expect an answer from her husband.

"Why did she have to leave?" Efemena asked.

"Her husband is late. Therefore she cannot remain in the women's wing." Enatomare sat down.

"But why?"

"That is the law of the progressive meeting. If a man dies, his wife is automatically dismembered."

"But if a woman dies, the husband remains?" Efemena probed.

"Yes," Enatomare said.

"I thought the association is a progressive union?" Efemena asked.

"Mena, if the man stays, his new wife will belong," her father responded impatiently.

"What if the woman marries another man, will she stay?"

"That is if Jessa remarries from our state. And if he independently joins our club, yes, she has a place again."

"Oso, if I am not mistaken,you are an advocate for women's rights. What if she desires to remain a member of the club?"

"No she cannot without an indigenous husband."

"But, you were in support of the equality bill that women should have as much rights as men in the society." Efemena was shocked by her father's stance.

She realized that her father only entertained her beliefs as childish fantasy. Now he told her his truth.

"Feminism ends in the book, Mena. That is why your relationship is not working. Get me some pepper soup, lady, bring it to my study, thanks." Efemena looked at her mother for solidarity, but Enatomare was helpless.

✻   ✻   ✻   ✻   ✻

The town appeared unrustled for the big event holding today. Most people were going about their daily activities. It was also a remarkable day to make good sales as tourists and guests flooded the community for the Sango Festival's grand finale. Most indigenous people appeared more interested in displaying their commodities to attract patronage. Efemena drove into the premises after been searched by the mobile police at the gate.

The Sango festival had been in existence for over a thousand years, but was redesigned to World Sango Festival with all its sacred colouration for international recognition, indigenous and individual awareness. It is one cultural practice that cannot go into extinction because if there is no Sango, there is no Alaafin. If there is no Alaafin, definitely there would not be an Oyo kingdom.

Efemena delivered the items to the Olori's chamber and decided to enjoy the festival. She paid rapt attention when the spectacular presentations of the festival commenced. Sacrifices were made to Sango, as they offered ram, amala (yam flower) and other items to the deity. In ancient mythology, Sango exhibited his magical prowess at the feast. He cut out his eyes and blood dripped. He also rammed a six-inch nail into his forehead with a hammer and pranced with agility feeling no pain as he extracted the object from his head which drew screams from spectators frenzied and frightened at his performance. Acrobatic dances, and drama were performed by various cultural groups within and outside Nigeria.

The dramatic Sango temple was painted red and the devotees wore red clothes and plaited their hair mostly in cornrows. The devotees consisted of males and females; children were not left out as they publicly declared that they were Sango's devotees. These devotees never belonged to the western religions of Christianity or Islam. In the temple were many benches where they congregated every Saturday to worship just like in any church. They had been born into the servitude of Sango as each generation, husbands, wives, and children succumbed to the worship.

Members of the community were well protected against thunderbolt because they worshipped Sango. Nobody dared–indigene or non-indigene to steal a property of Sango and whenever lightning flashed and thunder roared, the Sango worshippers shouted, "the king did not hang himself!"

The drama ended with a standing ovation from the guests, and loud cheers filled the air as Pamela, the cultural ambassador to the Alaafin, took over the stage to commend the expertise in their performances. She highlighted that the major reason for the celebration and continual worship of Sango is to preserve the heritage and revitalize the intangible elements of Oyo Empire. Another reason for the projection of the Sango festival is for the United Nations Educational and Cultural Organizations to acknowledge the Sango festival as a heritage of the Yoruba race. Pamela added that concerning the ancient shrines that were destroyed, the Alaafin was taking necessary steps to have them rebuilt as some ancestral and generational rulers were attached to the religious rites that came with the festival.

With the thoughts of travelling in the new car she just ordered, Efemena drove out of the premises while Pamela's voice boomed from the loud speakers mounted at strategic canopies in the palace. She was saying that due to loss of cultural norms and values in major African communities, in the future, some people may have to travel to western countries in order to align with their heritage.

✲ ✲ ✲ ✲ ✲

Efemena travelled to Abia in the new car she bought. She drove carefully through cities conscious that she was alone in the car. Her music player was on and kept her company. She resumed unofficially at the private day and boarding school she was posted to. At her first glimpse of the school, she wished she had allowed her father use his influence on her posting. She ruled out the thought, taking it as fate. After all, she had prayed and asked God to choose for her place of primary assignment, a place where she would have peace and rest of mind. With that conviction, she had submitted her posting letter. She was ready to contribute her quota in imparting knowledge in the students and make her stay worthwhile in the best ways possible.

Efemena decided she could not live in the accommodation provided by the school. She was allergic to bushy areas; the fear of animals mostly snakes and insects or any other crawling thing when encountered left goose bumps on her body and at night, recounting the images frightened her and made her unable to sleep. She discovered these phobias the few times she had visited the village as a teenager. It was definitely not manageable. Opposite the school was a large asylum which was scarcely fenced with rusted iron, cement blocks cracked to a level it could crumble with just a kick. Sources said the patients were in critical derangement. The lodge was opposite the student's dormitory and adjacent the classrooms of the senior students. The rooms were fashioned out of classrooms. The bathroom was located few miles from that area. Teachers shared the bathrooms with the students, but a toilet was reserved for them. How she would tread those parts each day to have her bath and excrete was unimaginable to Efemena. She would have to wrap the towel around her, fetch water at the general tap, and carry the bucket to the bathroom. These processes would show her body to the whole school, her students, the same teenagers she would be teaching would have seen her bare. What if some of the boys stared at her thighs? It would be stupid and unhygienic to wear her clothes to the bathroom, and after washing, put them on again.

Efemena decided to get an apartment in town, where she could easily access better roads, do her shopping, make her hair, hang out with friends at good eateries and make better connection for her fashion business. She had paid an agent who showed her around and finally settled for a self-contained apartment.

The principal had nursed the idea that Efemena would be the hostel mistress for the girls and take the duties of the matron who was due for delivery and maternity leave. But with her opting to stay in town, she had disrupted his arrangement. He decided to teach her a lesson. He became cold and unfriendly after Efemena told him her plans. Efemena ignored his indifference, after all, he was not footing any of the expenditure.

The school resumed from the first term holiday. The staff had a meeting and the principal implored the teaching and non-teaching staff to recommend the school to family and friends. He commended their positive impact on the pupils, morally and academically and chastised the matron for not being vigilant as some students made phone calls in the hostel. It was while the principal was talking that Efemena came in. The principal ignored her and continued his speech. When the principal finished addressing the staff, Efemena apologized for coming late, explained that there was a long queue at the fuel station, and a little traffic jam caused by herdsmen and their cows. The teachers and other staff murmured while the principal, with the wave of his left hand asked her to sit. After a while, the meeting ended and they left. Efemena offered to drop some of the staff who were going her way off.

On the first day of resumption, Efemena was early enough.

She arrived at the vice principal's office to collect textbooks, notebooks and other writing materials. Whilst waiting, the principal came in and asked her to see him. He did not take her to his office but the school's library, where he told her of his decision to reject her.

Efemena was shocked but masked her disappointment behind her smiles. She wanted to ask him why he rejected her after accepting her posting letter. Maybe this is a great turn, since he was the one rejecting, it was no crime. If she had opted for it, it would be a penalizing offense by the NYSC laws which states that a corps member should not push for rejection at his or her place of primary assignment.

She did not ask him for his reasons but agreed to the rejection. She requested for the letter but was told it was not ready. She was to come on Monday. She thanked him, exited the library, bade her colleagues goodbye in the staffroom, and left the premises. In her car, she breathed a sigh of relief. Satisfaction was written over her face. "At last, I am finally free from here." Although she was disappointed, she consoled herself. "I believe everything is working out for the best." Efemena sped down the bush path into the tarred road. Since she was not going back to the school, she used the rest of the week to buy some furniture, called a painter and carpenter and furnished the apartment: the place she would call home for the next ten months.

Efemena was lucky to find a catholic church not too far from her house. She decided not to drive to church but walked there instead. While in church, her prayers were to successfully collect her rejection letter and find a suitable place of primary assignment around the town.

Efemena got to the school the following Monday to pick up her letter. She unfolded the paper and scanned the content. She was weakened. In the letter, the principal stated he had rejected her at her request due to her lazy attitude and her unwillingness to serve. Tears gathered in her eyes. She wondered why the principal would write such a letter. She wanted to go back and confront him but her legs would not carry her. She wobbled to her car and drove to the corpers' lodge. The lodge was a bit calm compared to the first time she and her batch had arrived from the orientation camp. It was like a mini barrack with corps members in uniform. The lodge was empty because corps members had resumed at their various places of primary assignment. Only those posted to the local government resided in the *corpers'* lodge. When she sauntered into the building, she felt at home forgetting her worries for a moment. The lodge had a master's bedroom and four other rooms, two toilets and bathrooms. The sheds outside were constructed to form a hall for Christians and a praying ground for Muslims. The veranda was protected by a secured net guard. From the kitchen, a door led into another apartment with a store room, a toilet and bath, and two bedrooms. The store was used by Mamo, the spiritual mother of the Christian *corpers* fellowship, to sell drinks.

Once in every three months, corps members were mobilized into three batches: **A, B,** and **C.** These three batches must rotate and stay for a period of a year except circumstantially it was altered for state or national security reasons. Efemena's batch had met the batch **C** and **A**. The batch **C**, the oldest had virtually the best of everything in the house. The appointed corps liaison officer either male or female occupied the best room in the lodge. Efemena and her batch met the male CLO. The master bedroom was taken by the CLO, and few males who had offices in NCCF and MCAN. The first room opposite the master bedroom housed their female counterparts. The other corps members shared the remaining rooms. There was no power supply but for the grace of '*I better pass my neighbour*' generator to charge phones and laptops. The meals served barely went round and some had to sleep on empty stomachs that grumbled nosily later at night.

Mamo and other business entrepreneurs advertised their catering services on papers pasted around the lodge. Their list read: noodles and egg, bread and tea, pure water, soft drinks, recharge cards, with a side note that, after meals, eating utensils should be washed and kept in their appropriate places by each individual, and that the kitchen should be kept tidy at all times by making good use of the trash can. *'Thank you and God bless as you comply.'* The lodge's entrepreneurs had great sales when new corps members came because they were, *'Jonney Just Come'* and did not have alternatives than to buy their goods at whatever price. They were new to the environment and did not know their way around.

Efemena hauled greetings at the people in the house and engaged in small chats. Few corps members were still having problems with accommodation and stayed back while they searched for better places. There was a case of four corps members posted to same place of primary assignment. A girl and three males were posted to a school in a village where they would have to cross over with canoe anytime they were attending CDS or had tasks to do in town. The girl did not like the environment, she devised means to get rejected by the principal but her tactics failed. The woman knew most tricks orchestrated by dissatisfied corps members like acting deaf, dumb, all forms of disabilities. She feigned being an imbecile, still the principal accepted. Two days in the act, she could not keep up with the drama; she claimed she had been healed by a minister during a vigil at the village hall. The principal had shouted. "Hallelujah, what a great miracle!" She tried not to laugh.

After exchanging pleasantries with some corps members, Efemena went in search of the CLO who might have a remedy for her plight. The CLO was displeased with the content of the letter, and angry at whatever reasons the principal had for drafting such disastrous text. He was busy dealing with other such matters and could not leave his desk, he pleaded with a colleague to accompany her to the school and beg the principal to reconsider his stand in the letter which could hinder a successful service year.

The purpose of the trip was defeated as the principal blatantly refused, insisting that Efemena had what she asked for. The principal stated that she indirectly asked for it when she went ahead to rent an apartment in town, causing her to come late for the school meeting, and would probably have more excuses for coming late every other day. He was not ready to upset the organization with her crooked excuses of queuing at the fuel station or traffic jam on the way.

"Oh! So that is what this is about?" The corps member who had accompanied her was amused and angry at the same time at the principal's lame reasons. After that, all pleas proved futile, they stood up, thanked him, and headed to the lodge. Back at the lodge, the CLO was displeased at the principal's shallow disposition. He could have approached him, but he did not have the time. He would have gone if not for anything, but to lecture the man not to write false statements against corps members. He told Efemena to put a call to the local government inspector and tell her that she had been rejected by her proposed employer.

Tuesday morning was the appointed date for clearance. Every corps member was to obtain a clearance letter from their employers, and the money would be paid into bank accounts opened and sponsored by the federal government. Corps members who had been cleared in their various offices and schools were happy at the prospects of receiving alerts. Efemena had a different predicament. She had neither a place of assignment nor a clearance letter. She plastered a fake smile on her face as she greeted her friends.

Efemena had been nervous since morning. She was worried about her fate; a month after orientation, she had no place of assignment. The CLO had told her not to get on the normal queue, but to stay aside and pray the inspector was in a good mood and agree for her to be reposted after listening to her case.

The LGI was in her early forties. She was beautiful and intelligent and exuded elegance and style. Mrs Obia Abigail, the local government inspector would go to any length to see that corps members were settled at their various places of primary assignment and their rights were not denied them. There was a case of a private school proprietor who refused to pay three months' salary to her Batch **C** corps members. She had stormed the principal's office threatening to withdraw them, and never to forward their request letter to the orientation camp whenever corps members were mobilized. This was one thing most of such employers do not take likely as these corps members offer them cheaper labour than regular staff. In less than three days, the affected members were paid.

Efemena silently prayed to be forgiven in any way she had erred in the matter. After the clearance, Mrs Obia had assessed the reports of the CDS groups. She was satisfied with their reports and commended their efforts. She was in a good mood; Efemena was happy. As Mrs Obia proceeded to her car, the CLO beckoned Efemena to move closer. The CLO presented Efemena's case to the local government inspector. Just when she would reply, her phone rang and she had to leave.

In a hurry, she chastised Efemena for getting rejected so late and asked to see the rejection letter. Whilst Efemena was looking for the letter, Mrs Obia's phone rang again. She instructed the CLO to collect the letter and post Efemena to another place. Efemena was excited. She thanked and prayed for the CLO. With the influence of the CLO, she was posted to the local government office. The chairman, a man in his early forties had obliged him because he felt concerned and did everything to make corps members at ease. With his office, he ensured that Efemena's name was added to the payroll of the local government area.

Seven

Chinwe ascended a slopy rough neighbourhood carpeted with dirt and dust after winding off the interlocked road that led to a busy street. Commuters made their way in and out, blaring horns from motorcycles and tricycles deafened the atmosphere. Words flew around like controversial football analysts in a non-stop segment from different radios.

A young man with begrimed dreadlocks sat on the bonnet of an abandoned truck. He stopped playing his guitar when Chinwe came up in front of him. The slight wind that wisped made her Buba dress billow like angel wings.

"Boyoboyo."

"My fine madam."

"How are you today?"

"I thank Jah for sparing my life. So, I fine, Ma."

Chinwe knew he was looking bad, her smile was sad. "Me see you fine well-well."

"What of your family? My friend has come back from school?"

"No he is not back yet. He would be back for mid-term break this weekend. You will see him then, Boyoboyo, he misses your songs."

He nodded. "You are going to church. I see your big Bible."

She clasped the big King James Bible to her bosom. "Yes, there is choir practice today."

"Someday, when me hale, looking good. I go play and sing

thunder firing songs to heaven."

"Yes, Boyoboyo. You will join us every Sunday."

"Me hope for that day, Ma."

"Boyoboyo, take this for fruits okay." She pressed five shiny two hundred naira notes into his bedraggled palms.

"You are too much, my fine madam. God bless you." Chinwe left him sadly. She resolved to speak with her pastor today.

A figure laid flat at the altar, racking with heavy sobs. The dishevelled weave showed it was a lady's; she was not less than seventeen years old. She was crying so hard, but the sounds were muffled as she did not want to draw attention to her frail self, she only needed a moment with her creator to cry out her pains, mistakes, sorrows, realizations, repentance, as she sought refuge, salvation, wisdom, guidance and protection from the owlish world that awaited her after this holy peaceful sanctuary.

Her tears intensified, she removed the shawl around her shoulders and stuffed it into her mouth as she cried harder. She did not want to disrupt the choristers in their rehearsals. She thought her sinful voice should not be mixed with the pure words of the Holy Ghost.

The ladies occupying the first two pews raised their voices to chorus the glorious hymn of Hosanna in the Highest, and those words tore her heart. 'Blessed the sinner who cometh.' She did not know when the words left her mouth, she began screaming.

"Oh God, my heavenly father, please forgive me, have mercy on me, Lord, fan my soul with your air, light my heart with your heavenly sky, touch my soul with your spirit, free me Lord from this hurt that wages a battle in my heart."

The cry continued with the bewildered choir and some of the members in their weekly activities stared at her; confusion, pity and worry etched on their faces.

Chinwe approached the pastor after he concluded a meeting "Pastor?"

"Yes, Sister Chinwe." Some members exchanged greetings with the pastor and acknowledged Chinwe.

"It is about Boyoboyo," she went straight to the point.

"Boyoboyo?" He called the name like he had never heard it before.

Chinwe glared at him. "Boyoboyo at the church junction."

"Oh! Aha, that brother the church is set to deliver?"

"Yes, Pastor Henry."

"Oh, Sister, do not think we have forgotten all about him. In fact, I have made arrangements with a psychiatric hospital that would administer treatment on him from this Friday."

"But, Pastor, as the head of the planning committee, you should have informed me of this development."

"Yeah, actually, I was going to tell you on Sunday."

"Did you say Sunday ,Pastor? You just said Boyoboyo would be taken into rehabilitation by Friday. How come you would have told me by Sunday?"

"Don't mind me, dear Sister Chinwe. You see, I meant to say, I would tell you today, after choir practice."

"Okay. Please can I have the address of the hospital, and contact number. I and some members can go over tomorrow to check their facilities."

"There will be no need for that Sister. By Sunday, oh sorry I mean Friday, we will see it."

"Okay, if you say so, Pastor. I will see him on Tuesday by God's grace. I'm attending a conference in Abuja from Saturday to Monday. I trust you have chosen one of the best hospitals."

"Oh I see. Safe journey when you embark on the trip."

"Yes, Pastor." She stood up. "I'll take my leave now. My regards to madam and the children."

"Oh and Sister Chinwe?"

"Yes, Pastor?"

"Bless you, my sister."

"Bless you too, Pastor."

"About the five split air-conditioners you pledged during our recent harvest. I want to remind you that you are yet to redeem it, and the church is urging you to do so. A promise is a debt."

"Yes, Pastor. I will after this project at hand. We might incur other costs. In case the money we have contributed so far is not enough, I might have to delve into my personal purse to execute it. So, I am waiting until we complete this project."

"That's kind and humbly generous of you. But, Sister, the air-conditioners are very important. We are losing brethren because the heat is becoming unbearable. The fans do not make the church conducive enough."

"We need to save a soul, do not talk to me about greedy people. Heat cannot kill them, but Boyoboyo's drug addiction can kill him in no time. He virtually spends every dime he has on weed. He is willing to stay away if he receives necessary medical attention. The disgruntled ones can import snow, heaven would not break."

"Yes, you are right. We will put a hold to that. But if it is possible for you to redeem two before then, it will be great."

"Okay, I will think about it. The bank is yet to disburse salaries and my account is virtually empty. I will ask my husband if he can assist."

"Oh that would be excellent, Sister Chinwe."

"Okay, bye, Pastor."

"May God enrich your pocket, Sister Chinwe. My humble regards to your husband."

❧| *Eight* |❧

Under the covers of the full moon, brightness shone on two people. She is really here, seated in front of him, he thought. The forceful effort to sneeze shut his eyes.

The lady quickly said, "Sorry."

On opening his eyes, he responded, "Excuse me please." He looked so boyish at the instant; tweaking his nose with a handkerchief he retrieved from his breast pocket.

Enthralled and in an elated fit, Efemena gave him a lazy punch on his left arm. "Wow, Ike! You are such an amazing man; I had a lovely time with you."

"Yeah, baby, I am glad you enjoyed yourself. I am happy too and hope we get to hang out more often from now on." Jamuike winked as he rubbed his arm.

"Yes we will. If our first date is this awesome, I bet others would be super. But, we will go out only if you do not allow that silly scenario to repeat itself."

"What scenario, how do you mean, baby?"

"You want to act oblivious? It is one bad habit I have observed but I bet you are faking it. Perhaps it is anytime you are around me because you are smarter than that. You acted like a punk back there at the restaurant." Jamuike gave her a bemused stare.

"The way you brushed that young man off was too harsh. You knew he waited for the tip. He is no less a man than you are. You rudely told him you could not give your penny to a fellow man."

"Yeah, I remember, and I still stand on that notion. I cannot give my hard-earned money to such a bloke, if he needs more cash he should get a better paying job. He should leave that act for the sissies, or get an extra job instead of "dog-walking" and pasting smiles like a beauty queen posing at a pageant."

"Don't say that, you can never tell if he has more than three jobs, or he is involved in businesses but still cannot offset his bills. He looked forlorn, like a starved kitten in need of milk. Maybe he was just desperate for those tips to buy water or anything. He looked like the tip could be useful."

"Whatever it is, that is his lot. Please can we just drop this, the guy is probably off duty, cooling off between his sweetheart's thighs or tapping his feet to the beats of the DJ's music. We should end this discussion."

He loosened his contorted features. "Please, Efemena, stop okay?" Efemena puffed her cheeks like balloons, her hands placed akimbo. Jamuike saw she was resolute and tried to redeem himself.

"Okay. I will practise the act of giving tips to anybody irrespective of gender and circumstance, if and when it is within my reach and capacity. Are you happy now?"

She sighed indifferently. "You are impossible. But then, it is better than nothing."

"Anything my love desires."

"Come off that! Who is your love? I beg your pardon, gentleman, I am not your love, and please do not call me such endearments."

"No qualms, if you insist, it is your call."

"Yeah. I insist, thank you." She smiled.

After some chirping silence, Efemena broke in, "Once again thanks for the treat."

"Don't mention. A queen like you deserves more, So, see you tomorrow at the office?"

"No seeing tomorrow, it's Thursday."

"So?"

"It is my CDS day."

"CDS?"

"Now you are at it again, you are such a bore. Yeah CDS, Community Development Service." Efemena scrowled.

"That's true."

"Obviously, it is." She snapped her fingers at his dreamy eyes.

"I wish you would not be absent every Thursday. I always miss your gorgeous presence."

"Well 'Mr Missing', it is obligatory I attend. It's my national duty, if I am not there; I will be made to pay a fee."

"How much is it and I will pay?" he asked with a pang of hope.

"That's not the point; it's not about the money. I may not be allowed to do my monthly clearance and I tell you, I cannot afford to lose my whooping nineteen thousand and eight hundred naira (₦19, 800). It is enough for peanut butter, bread, egg and noodles for two weeks before the next clearance."

"But then, you can come around the office after the meeting so we could spend some time together. I do miss you a lot. Say yes; please say yes you will come," he pleaded tenderly.

"Quit it, Jamuike. I have the whole day to meet and hang out with my fellow corps members I get to see once in a week. If not for the scheme, would you have ever set your eyes on me not to talk of us spending quality time together? I need to serve my fatherland, to interact with all kinds of people from various states and fields of study; that is my major priority and assignment."

"I am not saying you should not serve, do not get me wrong, I am only suggesting that you come over afterwards."

"Very well then, thank you for the suggestions. I cannot make it, even if I wanted to."

"Why?" Jamuike asked.

"The CDS has a project–a visit to an orphanage. I am the vice president of the Social CDS. I have to accompany my treasurer and financial secretary to the market to purchase some items for the kids. I will be very tired when I'm back."

"Alright, I understand. Such activities can be tasking, it reminds me of my own service year. Friday then, after duties we would go to the club and dance to relieve ourselves. I guess we will see on Friday then?"

"Yes, that is a great idea. See you on Friday, goodnight, Jamuike."

"Good night, my darling."

"Darling huh?"

"Good night, Efemena." He brushed his lips against her lips before she could stop him.

He clasped his hands together. "I'm sorry, ma'am, please do not slay me, my fair lady, I could not resist the urge."

Efemena smiled. "The deed is done." She opened his palms and dropped them at his sides. She smiled as she walked away. "This must be love."

"I'm going to have her, I wish badly to have her," he said as he got into his car.

When Efemena got home, the long bench was in its usual corner, precariously close to her bedroom window. "It seems these people are deaf or plain trouble makers." She had warned some of her neighbours, a particular set of girls, to stop putting the bench there. The compound was big enough to have it fixed anywhere, even the mango tree in the middle would make a cool spot for their studies or gossips. She had never seen such idle students in her life.

They stayed at home all day, went out in the evening and came back in the morning. Efemena resolved to see the caretaker first thing in the morning to complain. It was high time the girls told her what they wanted close to her bedroom.

Once inside the apartment, Efemena rested on the closed

door, placed a hand on her chest with the other clamped on the doorknob, and felt the fast beat of her heart anytime she left Jamuike's presence. She moistened her upper and lower lips with her tongue. There was something about him that made her feel there were birds singing in her head, their music was melodious but too dangerous to dance to.

✳   ✳   ✳   ✳   ✳

The secretary tried to stop Ada as she barged into the office and dropped her bag on his desk.

"I am sorry, Sir, I tried to stop her but she pushed me out of the way," the secretary said panicking.

"It is okay, you can go back to your desk."

"Okay, thank you, Sir." She gave Ada a cold stare as she walked out of the office.

"You fooled me, James, how could you?" She dragged some document off the table with her hand in anger.

"Wow, wow, calm down, baby, I can explain," he gestured with his hands.

"Don't you dare baby me, just shut the hell up, you two-faced lying dog."

"I never did such, and I take great exception to you calling me a dog."

"Oh shut up for decency sakes, a dog you are and a filthy one at that!"

James had become angry but tried not to show it, he rapped his knuckles gently on the desk. "I never lied to you, baby."

"You are a liar, how dare you make such a shameless denial after knowing the truth so well?"

"I never did."

"Yes you did. You did not tell me you are married."

"You never asked."

"What?"

"Yes, you never asked. Darling, I told you from the onset of our affair to ask anything you wanted to know about me, and all that you enquired, I did give you answers. I guess you did not care to know my marital status. I did ask of yours, you told me, and I am comfortable with it."

Ada placed her hand on her chest and sank into a chair. "Oh my God, oh my God, This is unbelievable! James, you are smooth. I would be lying to myself if I do not admit that I am a fool!"

"Yes, my lady, you've been fornicating with a married man, now you know."

"But, but you knew I took you to be a bachelor. I thought we were into a relationship that would lead to marriage. You never wore a wedding band."

"That is one mistake you made, sweetheart; I never assumed anything but always asked questions. My ring grew too small; I have been married for eight years. It's with a goldsmith."

"Oh! How could you have done this to me, James? I loved you, so why, why!" She was about crying.

"You did not ask, it is not my fault. If you had faced it, I mean if you had asked, I would have told you I am a happily married man and proud father."

"This day I see a clear mirror of a heartless man. James, you are a beast" she said sobbing

"And you are a pretty sweet beauty."

"I hate you so much," she gritted her teeth.

"And I love you so much, baby," he said with lust in his voice; staring hungrily at her big heaving bust.

"Oh just shut up! To hell with you, you are so full of shit." She spat on some documents on the desk.

"This should not be the end of our affair, truly I love you so much and you are my kind of girl."

"I will spite you forever for these insults. You know what?" Poking her heart, she said, "I too, I'm good enough to be somebody's wife and mother. Goodbye." She dabbed her eyes with the back of her palm and sniffed.

"Goodbye, Ada, best wishes, missing you already, really bad, will miss the warmth you offer. But you really should think things over, don't be so hasty with your resolve to break this beautiful relationship we have, we can make things work, baby."

Ada turned back to look at him, she shook her head then gave a loud hiss and exited the office. James smiled after she closed the door with a bang. He rubbed his palm together, licked his lips, and got working.

Ada ran into the compound, she rested her lithe body on the passenger side of Efemena's car and wept bitterly. Efemena heard her cry through her bedroom window and wondered what the problem was. She wanted to come and console the troubled lady, but Ada wiped her eyes and ran into her apartment.

⌘ *Nine* ⌘

ARUE CO. Oil Limited met with some prospective partners and clients to deliberate on a business proposal. Akpos headed the presentation with Adekunle, Mustapha, Chima and Bimbo in attendance.

"The federal government of Nigeria has said it no longer has the resources to fund the oil industry, but yet approved forty billion naira (₦40b) for oil exploration in the North at a time when the wiser decision was to diversify the economy to sectors like agriculture, science and technology. As it is, the militants, Niger-Delta Avengers, are not making the situation any better with the bombing of pipelines and oil facilities.

"The availability of Niger-Delta crude has greased the economy of the federation. The oil is considered very important with benefits that the ruling party are obsessed with winning elections in the oil producing states such as Delta, Rivers, Akwa Ibom, and Bayelsa. This is to say, oil power is obsessive, everybody wants their claws on it, but it is exclusive to the elite. Only the bosses at the top can venture into this business. Since we cannot own oil wells and blocs, why can't the middle scale businessmen and women tap into another sector that can boost economic revenues?

"Therefore, let's talk about the palm tree. A lot has been said and done about the palm tree; some of us grew up around it without any knowledge of its potentials. You might ask what goldmine it possesses. But, it generates about fifty-seven billion naira for an industry that keeps waxing stronger yearly from its production.

"Some of you know what I'm talking about. You might have parents and relatives who own large expanses of land flourishing with palm trees. But recently, many able-bodied persons have moved off to big cities in search of white collar jobs, ignoring the green pastures back home. Yearly, you head back home, only to use the trees as shade or lovers' spot.

"The fruit when processed, produces delicacies like Banga soup, palm oil for preparing soups, and other meals, palm kernel oil for soaps and creams, animal feeds, to roofing materials and the latest, brake-pads!

"Like seriously, that's fifty-seven billion naira business going to waste. When its resources are utilized, palm kernel in Nigeria is where most farmers make millions annually. Although, it can be a tough process trying to get the kernel out of its shell, it is gradually becoming a lot easier with machinery. It is a very lucrative business, one that pays thousands of naira per ton.

"Have you ever taken time to ask, what else we can get from the oil palm tree, and what they can be used for? Most times when I ask people, what other items they can get from a palm tree, aside palm oil and palm kernel oil, their usual response is the shell or chaff, that is if they have a market for it; while others will say 'nothing else'. Truth is, there is more you can get from a palm tree and they include: empty fruit bunches which materialize after the palm oil fruits have been separated from the bunch. After separation, they are usually wet. When dried they can be used as a source of fuel or returned to the plantation as decaying fertilizer for the palm trees.

"Palm fibres and palm kernel shells are the chaff and debris that come from shelling palm kernels. They are a good source of fertilizer used in melon and pineapple plantations. Palm kernel shells also extracted from cracking palm kernel, are a good source of fuel material for blacksmiths for their casts and forges when used in small quantities. It can also be turned into charcoal but tends to have high amount of impurities. It can also be used in making a light cement substitute material called Pozzolan.

"Let us serialize in simple terms the viability and profitability of this business on a small scale and for ease of understanding. The process of crushing palm kernel nuts will result in producing palm kernel oil, palm kernel cake and palm kernel sludge." Akpos scrolled through the slides to show his calculations.

"These are massive figures," a board member said and whistled coolly.

"Yes, however, the figures above tend to change frequently. What you see here was obtained as at the time of writing this report. It might not be the same now." His listeners were entralled.

At the end of his presentation, Akpos bowed and moved the cursor to each slide, and nodded when he reached the initial text.

"Hmmm, an eye-opener," a board member remarked.

"It's informative and educational. Villagers like us know the whole process on an individual scale but there is a huge market waiting to be tapped. Nigeria Institute for Oil Palm Research used to lead this effort in Nigeria; Edo State still has huge oil palm estates, some of which were planted during Ogbemudia's military government. The sad thing is that Indonesia came to NIFOR in the early seventies to learn the technological aspect of oil palm production and is today, the number one exporter of oil palm products. Nigeria drifted to crude oil and allowed everything else to fall apart. However, prospective investors will need a viable fifteen acre farm to get up to twenty-five tons of PKN. The cost of labour is killing and herbicide is very expensive when you look at the return on investment. Lack of proper regulatory authority engenders waste from the farm to the processing factory ... There are tales of woes when it comes to actualizing the beautiful presentation," he added.

"This presentation is not about owning a plantation and, besides, there are tales of woes in every business," Akpos highlighted.

"In this case you don't need to worry about planting, fumigating and the rest. The trees you will be harvesting from, have been planted a long time ago and you can harvest it for an even longer time," A client remarked.

"Another good thing is that, what you called waste, due to poor or improper regulation is now sellable and locally too," Bimbo chipped in.

"That's the grey part of the business. Existing plantations are not viable given their ages, in Ogun, Osun, Edo and Cross River States. With the exception of the big plantations of the established multinationals and public companies who are more or less conduits, there are not enough palm kernel nuts to fulfil the present processing demands of palm kernel oil," Mustapha noted.

Adekunle replied Mustapha, "There is more to it practically than the presentation. Presently there is scarcity of palm kernel nut and we go as far as Togo to source. Production is uneconomical and processing few is like a pseudo-monopoly being dominated by Presco and two others."

Chima responded. "There may be an initial supply challenge with palm kernel nut in the short run because of barriers created by the pseudo-monopolists. But in the long run, the supply chain will accommodate others. Monopolistic competition in the agricultural sector doesn't last."

"Let us be mindful of the quantities I used for this illustration. Forty tons of palm kernel nut in six days is conveniently attainable," Akpos reiterated.

"Please, excuse me, I have to take this call." Akpos waved his phone as an indication and went out of the conference room.

"Yes, Sir, the meeting is going well. So, I think we should move now to acquire acres of land in the village. They are very fertile."

He smiled to his father's response. "Yes, we can scale through any challenge; this business is a good bet. Okay, thank you, Sir."

$$\star \quad \star \quad \star \quad \star \quad \star$$

Nawg is a beautiful community with great landscape and good structures; both old and new. The good number of industries, banks, manufacturing companies, and the state university situated there made it a small metropolis. It was normal for the local government secretariat to be packed on Monday mornings.

Many court cases were held and judgment passed; which were either favourable to one or fair to both parties. Fleets of cars lined carelessly, tricycles jammed like bicycles queued ready for the Olympic race. Sidewalks housed various merchants advertising their wares. The local government junior staff as well as some of the senior staff seized the busy day to display their goods.

The commodities were trays of perishable and imperishable goods; pepper, tomatoes, plantains, bananas, vegetables, onions, palm oil, fruits, dried fish, bush meat, clothes, bags and shoes, amongst others. The dealers were patronized because what they offered for sale boasted of quality, especially the pepper which is locally grown, devoid of fertilizers, giving it a sweet natural taste, red oil extracted from fresh palm nuts, river fishes-dried no later than twenty-four hours, meat hunted by lion hunters and trappers who knew the forest like their big toes. Cheap fruit plucked from private healthy farms, affordable jewelry that had lasted scores of years and could still last for a great deal of time with its new owners. The least items that did not have high sales were foot wears.

Attached to the security post was a cobbler in his late fifties named Pa Uzoma. He was a genius when it came to making men's footwear and unisex slippers. Some of his clients bought the materials and trusted him to make handsome designer shoes. His products could pass for imported pairs, the only difference was the lack of label designs.

Amidst the bustling of the LG's heart, numerous court proceedings were on. The magistrate court, five miles from the bywalks, was alive with cases to be discharged, adjourned, or acquitted through the nooks and cranny of the law by the judge, plaintiff or defendant.

The district judge presiding was Justice Charles Arinze. He was a renowned advocate of the law and a humble patriot of the whole community. He believed that no man, irrespective of status quo, was above the law. But the cow, however big, was bullied down the fields to eat elephant grass or weeds, consume water from any pond as long as it is drinkable and at the sound of a whistle, it rears its heads on to the directed paths it has been commanded. One good attribute of his was to see justice served within his capability.

So many case files were announced and dealt with easily. The toughest were usually on the issue of landed properties. A man had died bequeathing his vast land assets to his son. While his corpse laid cold in the morgue, the uncles and siblings, distant and immediate relatives contested the ownership with the wife and son. Another case was that of a young man, a philanthropist, who had temporarily given a land to a school proprietor. The older man claimed ownership of the plots after years of his benefactor's absence from the country. Before the matter was brought to court, the school was not fenced but in less than a week after the suit was filed, the proprietor had hurriedly built one.

The judge resolved the saga with no hassles. He knew the land originally had been given to him without cost, to run his business for some duration of years, after which he would evacuate the property. As an elder community man who had lived all his life in this town except when he went away for vacation and studies abroad or for engagements within the country's shores, he was abreast of the past and present issues in the community.

The absence of a legal agreement between both parties made the case a bit complicated. When the plaintiff noticed blocks had been erected, he hired bulldozers to pull down the walls.

When the defendant was prodded on what had crashed the fence same day of its finishing touches, he confirmed the plaintiff tumbled it.

The judge pronounced that only an authorized official could, with the power from the state, contract the demolition of an illegal structure and also, only a true owner could pull down a fence without permission.

The proprietor in fear of a lost battle, countered his earlier affirmation, and said it was demolished by rain and thunderstorm coupled with wild wind that collapsed the fence. The plantiff was declared the owner of the land and the defendant was fined the sum of a hundred thousand naira (₦100,000) as compensation to the accuser for summary offense and he was to foot the bills of his attorney.

Jamuike Akuabia was privileged to be acquainted with many personalities in the community. He was the court clerk at the local government. He felt he was as important as the dignitaries in his community. He had a comely appearance and attracted a lot of ladies to himself. He had the model figure – the six feet height and six packs appropriate for an athlete.

The attractive thirty-eight-year-old man wore a round-necked black polo, hugging his body, a white blazer, brown chinos trousers and polished Italian shoes. After attending court sessions all day, he stepped out for fresh air. The heat in the courtroom was suffocating; the six fans hanging from the ceiling were beyond repair. The armless chair with no backrest wrecked his back. He felt like a farmer who had ploughed at his farmland from sunrise to sundown. His long legs were aching; he had folded them underneath the small desk. As he stretched his body, he spotted the beautiful and gorgeous Efemena Aruegodore.

"Wow, she is so pretty. I feel like holding her in my arms," he said to himself, and winced at the strong agreement from his manhood.

He watched as she walked to him; she did not come to work

last Friday. He had waited for her and called her phone severally. The only thing that had stopped him from driving to her house was that she did not like intrusion and he did not want to get in her black book. "Morning, Mena."

"Good morning, Jamuike. How are you? Hope you did not miss me too much?" she asked.

"Of course, I missed you. All the trees over there," he looked over his shoulder at the thick forestation, "can bear witness because they felt my loneliness as I strolled here. The songs from the birds were my company." Efemena giggled and blushed.

"Why didn't you show up? Your phone lines were not reachable and my messages were not delivering on WhatsApp. You had me worried though I was convinced that you were fine wherever you were. The glow on your face confirms that. You did not miss me a bit I guess."

"I did miss you. We were busy with CDS project. We stayed awhile playing with the kids, presented our little token and took pictures with them. Jamuike, you should have seen these babies and toddlers, they are so cute and adorable; I did not want to leave. I felt like adopting them, if I could I surely would have," Efemena said emotionally.

"It was a great project. I can picture it vividly, it's really pathetic seeing those kids deposited in the arms of kind strangers by hit and run boyfriends and girlfriends, denied paternity and maternity bond who knows perhaps forever, and of course by the searing cold hands of death gripping their parents."

"Yeah..." she said sadly.

"We had a case about two months ago of a twenty-six years old lady who in the middle of the night had gone to the outer latrine to deliver. After the birth of her baby she put him inside the pit toilet, quickly cleaned up herself and covered the hole with a wide plank. It was not until the early hours of the morning when a neighbour, who went to relieve herself, discovered the breathing baby to the glory of the Almighty."

"Christ!" Efemena exclaimed. Goose bumps popped on the

surface of her skin. "That was devious, a spurn act from hell."

Jamuike continued in earnest agitation. "The lady cried out alarmingly, waking the compound. The toilet was broken to rescue the baby. He was adorned with various sizes of maggots and excrements."

"That girl should be thrown into the deepest soak away pit for eternity," Efemena said bitterly.

"She was arrested, the baby sent to an orphanage. As I speak to you, she is serving a jail sentence for attempted murder. She had pleaded mercy, claiming she didn't want to have her second child in poverty, her mother caters for her first child and she can't tell the father of this newborn."

"Very good, serves her right for such heinous crime," Efemena hissed with a tiny remorse for the lady's fate. "Jamuike, enough of your court's episodes, they're often so disheartening. I have to go in now to report at my desk and plead for unapproved absence to my supervisor."

"Good! That brings me back to that issue. What really happened to you?"

"Yea, Jamuike, it was a fun Friday still. The local government chairman coincidentally was visiting a sick relative at the same Crystal Angel's hospital where we were. He happily commended our positive initiatives, and assigned his personal assistant to organize for a venue. We were asked to converge at Brent Hotel and Resort where he had given orders to the manager to give us our requests."

"That's generous of him," Jamuike said.

"We got drinking and eating in top merriment for a job well done. The chairman drummed into our ears, moral and philosophical words of advice, to be upstanding and outstanding youths in the society both at home and abroad. One of the things he said that still pounds in my head every minute of the day is: 'you cannot enjoy the leisure money can buy until it's your own cash to spend, not on the bill of another.' Hinting we shouldn't be carried away with the idea someone will always buy goodies to appreciate every work done, we're to take our minds away from such expectation. Rather, selfless service to humanity should be our priority."

"Bravo, that's one excellent advice. I like that, I fully subscribe to it!"

"On getting to my house, as usual, there was power outage. For real, Jamuike, I don't know what it is with that part of Chiego. Other parts have steady if not consistent power supply, except my own street. It is enveloped in total darkness at night; more like where witches and wizards operate. It beats me why the bad situation remains that way when there are prominent men and women who can single-handed remedy the bad pole which the power officials say is the sole problem. I'd little or no fuel therefore I couldn't run the generator."

"What are you trying to insinuate about the gathering of witches and wizards, Efemena?" Jamuike felt slighted with the demeaning assumptions of his community.

"Nothing, absolutely nothing, I'm just ranting endlessly based on the fact that the situation is annoying. I was too tired and fatigue spelt my full name, I badly needed the extra sleep. Let me leave you now, you were heading somewhere I guess?" Efemena asked.

"Yeah, I was going to grab some edibles at the canteen. Do you mind joining me?"

"I'd like to, I need to go see Mrs Comfort, apologize and I will meet you up. Thanks."

"Okay, see you there," Jamuike called out as she walked into the administrative block and he headed down to the cafeteria building.

Ten

By Sunday, Boyoboyo was not at the hospital. He died some days later.

"Have you seen Boyoboyo's body?" Akpos asked his wife who had just returned home.

"Body?" She heaved the laptop bag off her shoulder.

"Corpse, yes."

"No!" She closed her mouth with one hand and stretched the other hand as if to ward off her husband's statements.

You and your church failed, Chinwe. Boyoboyo's body is lying in front of your church. They found him dead by the door this morning. The church was not even opened for him."

"Nooooo!" she screamed and ran out. She bumped into Mama Onome and toppled a five litre bucket of ground tomatoes.

"Ah! Chinwe, you have finished me." Mama Onome placed her hands on her head and fixed her eyes on the pool of tomatoes on the floor.

"Oh, I'm finished! Akpos!" She headed to his flat.

Chinwe ran all the way out to the church premises. Health inspectors were at work. They were fitting Boyoboyo's corpse into an empty sack. She went towards the corpse refusing to believe it was Boyoboyo.

"Pastor?" She walked towards Pastor Henry who had just appeared from the church house.

"Boyoboyo?" she pointed at the corpse. "He is dead. How come? I thought he would be recuperating, by now. He should be in hospital. We were supposed to flush the drugs off his system."

"Sister Chinwe, calm down please. There was a little delay, it was postponed." He tried to hold her shoulder.

"You told me everything will be alright, that everything was going on well." She ran to the health officials. "Stop, stop, leave the body for us." She loosened the bag.

"You say wetin?" one of them removed her hands.

"Leave his corpse. Our church will handle it." She tried to stop them again."*Madam, abeg commot for here.* Please leave so we can do our job."

"Pastor, tell them to give us Boyoboyo's body."

"Sister Chinwe, let them do their job. Do not interfere. Jesus said let the dead bury themselves, did he not?"

Chinwe froze, her back was stiff. "What are you saying, man of God?"

"Let the government bury him."

"What, are you kidding me? This is no burial, Pastor. They will just dump him like waste.

"He is a waste, Sister Chinwe. Let it go."

"You will just let them take him away?" She pointed at the officials carrying him and ran to stop them.

"Madam, please allow us do our job or we would just leave it behind to pollute your neighbourhood," the driver said from where he was looking at the commotion from his rear mirror.

"Pastor, let us take him to the mortuary."

"He has no family, who would cover the expenses?"

"The committee would through his health funds."

"No, Sister Chinwe, we have invested that money into the church's event centre we are building. When it is completed, it will fetch the congregation revenues once we put it for lease."

"You said what!" She could not believe what she heard. "What do you mean, Man of God?"

"Please, gentlemen, carry on with your job. Thank you. Sis Chinwe, let us go into the church. You look worn out. How was your trip, Sister Chinwe? It took longer than you said." Chinwe stared in trance as they deposited Boyoboyo's corpse inside the bus and drove away. She gazed at the moving vehicle until it was no more in sight.

The activities that followed the rest of the week were less tedious. Most workers would come to work as late as 11 am and get off duty as early as 1 pm. It was the typical way government organizations were run by its officials. As soon as the boss exited the premises, the subordinates followed allowing the security personnel to act as chairmen for the better part of the day. For Efemena, whether Mondays or any other work days, she had less or practically nothing to do.

She was in the department of finance and her basic duty was to compile the employees' payroll. It was at the beginning of a new month that she got busy. Most times, the government delayed the pay of its officials, and oftentimes the salary earners were not perturbed because they had other means of livelihood which was the reason for their carefree attitude in their respective departments. It was the corps members posted to the local government that bore the whips of these government shortcomings. Their sustenance was on the peanut given to them by the state government. That was not the case with Efemena. She was from a well to do family. Her father was a businessman while her mother was a matron at a federal hospital. The only thing she lacked was the physical company of her parents and siblings. She had everything money could buy. She could have served close to her home, but she had declined her father's intention to use his influence. As a corps member, she sold clothes and foot wears to prominent people in the community, around the local government and to some of her corps members.

Efemena, on her way back from work, went straight to the caretaker's room. She had called him that she wanted to see him today; she was not buying the excuse of not being around or indisposed. He was not the only student that lived in the compound, or the most studious. Those girls were really getting her angry.

They did not even say hello to her. They only stared and gawked at her. She knocked severally at the caretaker's door but no response. Efemena thought of leaving but decided against it because the radio was on inside. She guessed people were in; there were shoes and socks on the mat outside.

"Hello, Dennis, it is Efemena, can I come in?"

There was no response. She turned to go but heard him say loudly, "You can come in now, baby, I am ready for you, please come right in."

"Huh! Even this one calls me baby too. These kids do not have respect; probably he thinks it is one of his babes. Dennis, well done, I'm now baby."

She stopped and gasped. "Oh, sorry, sorry, please pardon me. I thought you were calling me in. Oh, sorry, forgive me, I will come back." She turned and ran out of his room.

"Hey! These boys! What in the world was that, Dennis of all people, a gay?"

She closed her mouth and tiptoed towards her apartment. She had seen Dennis and a clergy who had a big church down the street making out on the floor, stark naked. What she had seen was so unbelievable, it would be hard for anybody to believe. She should just keep this to herself.

As she stepped out to go to work the next day, Dennis was by the passenger door of her car. "Good morning Efemena." He smiled and tucked his hands into his baggy trousers.

"Dennis, good morning. I did not see anything yesterday. You don't have to worry." She dangled her car keys.

"We cannot pretend it never happened, Efemena. Now you know I am homosexual," he said softly and exhaled loudly.

"Oh don't tell me. Just save me the details. I don't want to believe a brilliant young man like you is one. I mean … hum …

it should not be you."

"But you have seen that I am. It is in me and has become a part of me. I date men to get paid. I also do this because I love it." He chewed the gum in his mouth.

"It is so wrong, Dennis, all so wrong. Why are you telling me this?"

"Because I do not want you to judge me." He looked into her eyes.

"I do not have the right to but you know it is against God and the Nigerian law condemns the act. If you are caught, you will be jailed for fourteen years. Fourteen good years in prison, my dear!"

"I do not care. Mena, at this point in my life, I swear to you, I am not afraid of anything because of how hard life has dealt with me. Life has been full of crap. Growing up, I had big dreams and plans. But here I am today. Do not judge me, Mena. I was born with diamond spoons that glistered at every corner I turned to; it was pure heaven until I turned sixteen. And then, those clean spoons were snatched away; seems they have been locked away forever."

"What about your studies and family?"

"I do not have a family. I was disowned, and the reason is obvious. Well, do not worry. I will be careful until I leave for Europe. One of my friends is processing documents for me to come over."

"I guess it's a male friend right?"

"Yeah, I will leave after my graduation."

"And the national youth service?"

"I'm a part-time student. I will just get an exemption letter anytime the school is ready to issue one." He said the words flimsily.

"True, part-time students are not mobilized for service. But, Dennis, I believe you can fight this, just give it a try. You could see a psychologist or counsellor, anybody that can help you deal with this."

He shook his head. "Thanks but no, Efemena. I just need you not to tell anyone about this. I will really appreciate that."

"Dennis?" She held out her hands to hug him but he stopped her.

He ignored her hands. "Just promise me, please."

She exhaled and closed her eyes. "Your roommate, Michael, is he also homo?"

He became jealous as he clenched his fist tightly. "He is bisexual."

"Thanks, I thought as much, with the way he walks and the feminine colours he wears. I promise. Like I said earlier, Dennis, I never saw anything."

He gave a smile that did not reach his eyes. "Thank you. I am most grateful."

"You are welcome."

" Do have a splendid day. I will talk to the girls before the end of the day."

Efemena got in her car and revved the engine. He opened the gate for her, and she waved as she zoomed off. Efemena turned on the stereo, tuned to her favourite radio station and heard Mugabe saying, "Wake me after the speeches of Holland and Obama, if the next will be Cameron, let me continue my sleep. The Chinese and Russian speeches are enough for me. I don't want to hear the problem of lesbians and gays. Let's sleep my friends; sleep, is more important than the speeches of these clowns."

"Not again, Mugabe. This time we should not sleep, I want to disagree. We must all face and address this reality," Efemena lamented. The news ended and Bob Marley's 'Redemption Song' came on. Efemena sang and hummed as she drove to work.

Eleven

The week came to an end and Efemena looked forward to her night with Jamuike. He did not let her be until she agreed to go on a date with him. She stood in front of her gate waiting for him. Her neighbourhood was vibrant this night; people were either trooping into churches for vigil or clubs.

She was cold, even with a white blazer on, cold air seeped into her. Efemena wore a multi-coloured Ankara gown, cropped to her knees, a black suede wedge shoe, a small black purse in hand and pearl accessories. She stamped her feet to show her impatience. As she turned to get back into her cozy room, a car's headlight shone in her direction, it was Jamuike's. "Thank goodness, he is here at last!" Efemena almost screamed.

"Hi, baby! I am sorry for keeping you out here," Jamuike said coming out of the car.

"How dare you keep a lady waiting, Jamuike? When I called you thirty minutes ago you said I should give you ten minutes more, but it's over fifty," Efemena chastised him.

"My dear, I am sorry. I thought I should give you more time to put final touches to your make-up. You know how most ladies are."

"Well, I am not most ladies, I am Efemena Aruegodore." She hissed.

"Yeah I know, my precious, please don't get frustrated, okay." Efemena pouted. "Let us go. Our night is about to start, my lady, we should not spoil it," he said, smiling warmly.

"Alright, alright, get the door, will you, I am freezing out here," Efemena said.

"Oh pardon my manners, Miss, here we go." Jamuike bowed hurriedly as he opened the passenger door. He whistled as he sat in the driver's seat.

✧   ✧   ✧   ✧   ✧

Jasmine Bar was highly populated on Friday; all the lounges were filled. Efemena spotted an empty divan and led Jamuike to the spot. Everywhere buzzed with songs and reeked of assorted drinks. Jamuike went to place their orders; Efemena had requested for barbecued fish with chips. Jamuike brought two bottles of Vodka but Efemena declined the strong drink and asked for juice instead.

After eating, Jamuike brought out his wallet to pay the bills; Efemena held his hand and smiled. "I've got this, Jamuike," she said in a brisk and calm manner.

"No you wouldn't," Jamuike objected.

"Oh I would, you just watch me," Efemena said.

She paid the bills and tipped the waiter. Jamuike showed his displeasure at her gesture.

"You shouldn't have done that."

"Well I felt like it; just take it as my apology for standing you up the last time."

He kept his wallet. "Okay. If you put it that way. That's thoughtful of you."

"You are welcome." Efemena ran her hand through the creases on her dress.

They talked about the different dance steps they knew. Jamuike convinced Efemena to have a mix of brandy with her orange juice. She refused immediately but gave in after Jamuike teased her she was not able to hold her drink. She wanted to prove him wrong. Efemena became tipsy, she took more shots after the first and Jamuike did not hesitate to oblige her demands. Jamuike led her to the car and she slumped into the passenger's seat. Efemena had forgotten that her gate was locked by 11 pm. Unknowingly, Jamuike drove all the way to her house; the gate was already locked. The rules were strictly adhered to.

Efemena drunkenly asked Jamuike to take her to his own house. Jamuike felt like a fisherman who had caught varieties of shrimps. He had imagined getting intimate with her and the thought that tonight was going to be the night, made him carry out her request swiftly. "Thank God it is Friday," he murmured as he deposited her nicely at the back seat.

Jamuike's residence was male only, a bachelor to every apartment. The landlord in the past had had couples; married and courting who had series of fights that led to damaging of properties and police interventions. To avoid such chaos, he had refused to lease his house to married, or about-to-wed couples. The development allowed every male individual to own a key to the gate. So with ease, Jamuike opened the big gate, drove in and carried Efemena into his house. This part was different from Efemena's area, there was power supply. Still tipsy, she struggled to remove her dress asking Jamuike to undo her zip after which she flung herself on the couch and dozed off.

Jamuike was filled with longing; the full image of her naked flesh wrapped his mind. He was dazed by the peaceful beauty on his couch. She laid on her back, her full length under his burning caresses, he was just half feet taller and they would fit right lying together.

Her hair was plaited in thin long braids that dropped at her back and patted at her nape. He felt like planting kisses there, tracing his fingers down to her spine, his stare trailed down her back to her buttocks where it paused, and he gulped saliva at the sexy nature, fleshy like halves of a big water melon, her hips had enticing curves. She was moulded into fine perfection with long shapely legs. He inhaled deeply and turned away from her. "Holy crap! What am I doing?"

He moved closer this time and stretched out his hands to touch the nipple of her left breast that peeped out of her blue bra. He jerked before his fingers enclosed it; his eyes went below her stomach and fixed on her blue panties. He felt something heavy between his legs, looked down and saw his penis protruding in his pants, threatening to rip it off.

He took fast strides to his room, got in the bath and doused his body with cold water; the weather was cold which made the water cool and able to suppress his burning urge.

His senses would not take the appealing picture of Efemena off his mind, his penis had no pity as it ached and cried for relief. He ended his bathe in a hurry, dried himself and sauntered out of the bathroom. He fixed himself a shot of brandy and made his way to the living room where Efemena was asleep.

She looked uncomfortable on the couch; he debated whether to carry her into the room. He bundled her into his arms, down the passage, into the room and placed her on his bed.

Efemena's only reaction was to wrap her hands unconsciously around Jamuike's neck, as if she did not want to fall off. He laid beside Efemena after covering her with the duvet and shut his eyes like a schoolboy ordered by the headmistress as he fought himself to sleep.

Some minutes later, his eyes grudgingly opened; his body had registered the touch of a warm palm on his thighs and soft moans from a woman. Efemena was half awake, stroking his organ. He did not need any further invitation as he was drowned in hot passion for her. He got on her seductive form and unstrapped her bra. He scooped one luscious breast into his mouth to taste the sweetness of her nipples and hungrily cupped the other into his palm and massaged hard. Efemena wound her legs around his waist and caressed his back. They clung to each other in pure desire, kissing passionately. She had never imagined that he smelled this good as she inhaled his cologne. She felt his hand move up her thighs, fingering the walls of her sexual tissues; he had aroused her feminine sensitivity. His mouth remained on her lips, kissing, and sliding his tongue inside.

Jamuike became wild with need; he could feel his manhood so hard. With urgency he removed his boxers while Efemena pulled his shirt and then he helped her with her pant. He took one deep thrust inside and found her slippery wet, they moved in unison and in bouts of sexual bliss. They both had a massive cum amidst moans and groans.

Sated, they cuddled each other. Efemena drowsily gave way to sleep with her buttocks burrowed deep into his thighs. Jamuike stayed awake basking in the moment: "That was the best sex I have had in a while." He rained kisses on her back and smacked her buttocks lightly.

The rays of cool sunlight filtered through the window and slashed into the room. Efemena was the first to be conscious as her blurred vision recognised a male figure lying at her side. Her senses aligned with reality, in confusion she stared at Jamuike, took a glance beneath the covers and beheld her naked body.

"Oh Lord, oh my Goodness! Oh my! What have I done?"

Her outburst woke him; he huskily murmured greetings to her. "Good morning, honey." He dropped a soft kiss on her lips.

Efemena stared hard at him. "Jamuike, did we have sex?" she asked, praying he would say no.

"Yes we did, and it was so passionate," Jamuike affirmed romantically.

"Yes I know we did, and you say it so easily? Like it isn't bad enough, we had unprotected sex?"

"Well I am safe, and you?" Jamuike asked with a raised brow.

"Yeah, I am as well."

"Good, that means we are both safe and have nothing to worry about."

"Why would you utter such lame words? I could get pregnant you know."

"That would be great; I am ready to become a father."

"No, no don't be so positive. You sound so self-centred right now. I can't have a baby out of wedlock."

"Then I am ready to get married to you today or tomorrow, just say yes, baby."

"What!? Have you gone wacko? I barely even know you. I do not even like you."

"Oh but you just might, Efemena. Never say never, especially to one you have so much sexual passion for." Jamuike grinned.

"You lie, damn you are silly, don't be stupid. Where are my clothes? I need to get out of here." She turned around, looking for them.

"Without having your bath or breakfast?"

"I could care less. I have a bathroom and plenty of food in my own house. I don't want to be here longer than I have."

"Okay, but don't be too fast. You have forgotten that today is the last Saturday of the month, meaning no movement until 10 am and the time is just past seven. I advise you to have your bath then have something to eat; you must be famished after last night," he informed her with a victorious lopsided grin.

"Tell me where my clothes are."

"In the living room."

Efemena gathered the duvet around her body and walked to the living room. The door opened immediately and Emeka, Jamuike's neighbour stepped in. Emeka, a journalist had just been released from jail. He had published photographs of some government officials sharing money meant for national projects, in the commissioner for budget's office.

"Hey, Efemena, good morning." Emeka was shocked.

"H…i…Em…e…ka," she stammered. She was ashamed.

"I knocked severally but no one answered. So I came in thinking my man Jamuike was busy inside or something. I see he is really busy." He winked at Jamuike. "Jamuike, I'm sorry for barging in on you and your woman."

"I'm not his woman." Efemena retorted.

"It is okay Emeka, why are you here? Jamike interrupted.

"I came to ask you to borrow me your antivirus software, mine is out-dated and I am in the middle of a job."

"Okay, wait for me. I'll bring it to your room."

"Okay Jamuike, bye Efemena, have a great weekend." Emeka said as he walked away grinning.

Efemena sank to the ground; She was ashamed of herself. She had made herself cheap under Jamuike's cover. Nobody at work could have imagined they had sexual relationship but here she was. She wished this episode could stay within the walls. Around 8 pm, Jamuike went to drop her, the darkness shielding them.

They did not say a word to each other as he drove to her house. In her room, Efemena cried herself to sleep. Her pride was wounded.

❦| Twelve |❦

It was another Thursday and *CDS* day. Unlike other days, Efemena did not look enthusiastic. She felt like staying at home, doing nothing but drowning her mind in songs. The picture of having sex with Jamuike was still in her memory; she wished that it never happened. She avoided his face anytime their paths crossed. Finding a space to park her car was not funny. Her *CDS* group and two others had their meetings at a school. Today was its inter-house sports and vehicles and canopies filled every space. She was already frustrated.

She was not yet settled when the Chief Whip came to her to collect lateness fee. *Corper* Ubong was very meticulous; if any corps member was ten minutes late, he or she must pay the fine of fifty naira (₦50). Efemena was in for a lot of fines because she was inappropriately dressed. She wore a green sneakers to match her khaki instead of the traditional white tennis or jungle boot, which also attracted a fine of five hundred naira (₦500).

She was upset but she did not want Ubong's unwitty mode of pay what you owe or get a humming bird, he was an irritable nag when it was about money. She opened her handbag to settle the bills when the speaker for the day got her attention with his topic. It dawned on her that she had missed the greater part of his discussion.

The speaker, also a corps member was midway in his lecture. He was talking on the components of a good curriculum vitae. "So these are some steps for you to prepare your curriculum vitae as a fresh graduate. You might want to write them. It is important to provide a list of reachable contact options including your home address, your main phone number and your email address to enable prospective employers get in touch with you." The arena was silent as the speaker mentioned the vital steps to writing a CV. The corps members wrote the procedures on how to prepare a CV for a fresh graduate.

"Thank you so much. So far, you have done well. Most of us here strongly appreciate your effort on the topic you have shed light on today."

"Thank you, *Corper* Zainab. We hope for a favourable labour market that will accommodate the youths. So, ladies and gentlemen, hope your humble servant has made meaning from all he has been saying? And let me use this opportunity to inform you all that my first published book on how to write a comprehensive curriculum vitae would be available in paperback by next month. Lest I forget, it is my utmost pleasure to inform you all that the governor with permission from our NYSC coordinator, has approved our excursion within the state for this weekend. And the great news is … all expenses for the tour is to be paid by the amiable governor. Congratulations, ladies and gentlemen corps members!"

His announcement received cheers and many congratulations; he bowed and cautiously returned to his seat.

Other agendas of the meeting were discussed. The motion for the adjournment of the meeting was moved and seconded. The closing prayer was given by a Muslim corps member, as the opening prayer had been said by a Christian. They rose up to sing the NYSC anthem:

Youths obey the clarion call
Let us lift our nation high
Under the sun or in the rain
With dedication and selflessness
Nigeria is ours, Nigeria we serve.

At the close of the meeting, it was not the usual hanging around to chat. Corps members hitched themselves to those that had CVs in soft or hard copy and trooped in pairs to cyber cafés to make their own resumé, while those with laptops stayed. Efemena was not exempted, she had never thought of owning one until now, and she joined the cliques of CV writers.

✻   ✻   ✻   ✻   ✻

The crew had agreed to make Azumini Blue River, Azumini, in the ancient community of Ndoki, their first port of call. The sea of blueness and freshness made it a unique and an exquisite relaxation spot because there would be only a few people around in the early hours of the morning.

Named after its gorgeous sapphire waters, Azumini Blue River had stunning views of crystal clear water, surrounding beach and opportunities for canoe rides. It was recognized as the cleanest and clearest expanse of water in Nigeria, with easy to spot fishes swimming and darting on the water's surface. Each of the corps members settled down on chairs while their government escort went to clear the bills with the resort's management.

At that point, Efemena wished she had come with a blanket to spread on the beach to luxuriate in nature's splendour, and dive into the crystalline water in her naked form. She took a deep breath as the waves carried fresh breeze that wisped all around her. Now she could see why the Azumini River was acclaimed to be one of Nigeria's clearest blue water, as lush green trees cascaded around its cool blueness.

As they were about to leave, Efemena became envious of the inhabitants of the community. The kids played; diving hard and jumping into the blue water as it became wild and tumultuous. She shared open admiration at their young boldness as they dared the majestic swift waves.

Efemena marvelled at the breath-taking recreational site, a

108

land with spectacular scenery, wishing they did not have to leave and could pass the night right there on the beach. But her greediness made her forget so soon; they were heading to the War Museum at Umuahia.

Efemena descended the Azumini Hill from where she climbed and viewed the glaring beauty of the beach. She hoped someday she could come back with her family and leisurely savour the full pleasures the blue river offered. She noticed local and international tourists as they began to troop in with their cameras, tripods, food, and set grills. Traders made up their stands to roast corn, yam, plantain; tapsters hung gourds of fresh palm wine, amongst many other delicate fingerpicking snacks and meals.

The crew listened as the boatman that had taken them in his boat explained that the forebearers that discovered the river rested on the hill from which vantage point they glimpsed the alluring blue river and the fertile soil that blended it to nature's choicest settlement. They had come down the hill, crossed the blue sea and settled like the clan of Abraham in a promising land, but this time, it was the community by the river–Azumini River.

The corps members were elated about their next visit to National War Museum and Ojukwu's Bunker that housed the famous shortwave radio, 'the Voice of Biafra' which transmitted live from the horse's mouth during the Biafran war.

The National War Museum had the highest collection of the Nigerian civil war weapons no longer in use. There were weapons from both the Nigerian military and the defunct Republic of Biafra.

The environment seemed uncared for, though it was undergoing renovations. Their escort explained to the management and they were allowed free entry instead of paying the entrance fee of two hundred naira each. They were not ushered into the building until a small generator was put on to generate electricity. Everyone of them dropped their bags at the reception; phones or cameras were not allowed in, just writing pads. A tour guide took them to the prehistoric war section where some weapons were on display.

On display were spears, shields, bows and arrows; metal war vests that past warriors used to protect themselves as well as many other charms and amulets. They were led through the various rooms and the end of war weapons section led to the Nigerian Armed Forces gallery. There, the ceremonial uniforms of the army officers and the pictures of some past leaders were lined according to rank and the years they reigned.

They drove to the bunk house area. News had reached the management that some corps members were visiting, but they were adamant and insisted cash payments would be made. They had to pay fees before gaining access to the historic house that housed the Radio Biafra of the defunct republic. At the entrance, the Biafran flag of red, black, and green colours with a rising sun was hoisted.

A powerful Igbo proverb says 'a man who does not know where the rain began to beat him, cannot say where he dried his body.' The awareness of one's history determines the level of knowledge, interest and participation in present and future national or community affairs. It was a guide through what was, and a review of what should be and not be.

❧ *Thirteen* ❧

The weeks rolled by. Every activity took it usual course. A favourable period began for Efemena; her business was making huge progress. She had some of her goods sent from various states by her dealers. On arrival, she distributed the items customers requested and received payments in cash or cheque. With most of the goods distributed and sold, she carried the little in her possession to the office, CDS meetings, and to other establishments. After the incident at Jamuike's house, they barely said 'hi' to each other and since they were in different departments they were able to avoid each other.

Three months after the preceding corps members passed out, another set of prospective corps members were set to arrive at the NYSC orientation camp. Efemena planned to take a two-week permission off work as her presence had been formally requested at camp by the PRO, because she was a member of the Orientation Broadcasting Service, OBS and served as chief duty continuity announcer then. She and the former OBS crew would train the new recruits who would handle the activities of the studio with guidance from the PRO and other NYSC staff.

A day to the official opening, Efemena and other OBS crew members embarked on the journey to the orientation camp. On the road, they talked about their experiences on camp and their various places of primary assignment. Some succumbed to sleep, others operated their mobile gadgets taking shots of unfamiliar scenes. Efemena plugged her headphones and played the song

'East to West', even though this time, she was travelling East to East. When they arrived at the camp, they were not interrogated because they had evidence of being corps members. They were dressed in their NYSC uniform with identity cards and OBS crew tags. They were granted access into the camp and the bus stopped at the administrative building. They burst into the studio where they had spent time educating, informing and entertaining the camp. Efemena smiled seeing her initials and state code on the wall in the studio written with a permanent marker. They met with the camp officials and had a meeting on the activities on camp.

When batch **C** corps members arrived, it was a flurry of activities for Efemena and her crew. They were in charge of running the studio with guidelines and directives from superior staff. They took charge of broadcasting on the parade ground the first few mornings airing news at intervals, making general announcements pertaining to camp instructions and presenting live shows on various topics of human interest. They sold forms for interested candidates into OBS and conducted tests and interviews. They pasted the names of the qualified applicants; and began training so that they could take over from the present OBS crew.

Efemena could not stay through the rest of the week; she became sick suddenly. She was disappointed she would miss the pageants and competitions of Mr and Miss NYSC, Miss Hot Legs and Mr Macho, Miss Big Bold and Beautiful, the presentation of awards, the camp fire night, the long queues to sign the Book of Life and above all, the passing out parade by the corps members from orientation camp. Efemena thought she hadn't heard any ugly incident.

During her time, a newly wed lady had been caught having sex with a male corps member. Her husband was informed of her promiscuity and he brought along to the camp, her belongings and divorce papers to avoid her stepping her adulterous feet into his home. Another lady who had removed her expensive gold engagement ring in order to flirt but lost it in the process and cried almost every night for fear of what her suspicious fiancée would do to her when he discovers. She would laugh at corps members crying because they were posted to Nawg until they arrived and saw corps members wholly at peace in the community.

Fourteen

Efemena needed to go home; she had trained the new recruits assigned to her on how to ensure the smooth running of the studio. Recently she became tired easily, and at times felt dizzy. "I need to get good medical care, the camp's clinic barely has drugs other than Paracetamol and Vitamin C for whatever ailment the patient has," she sighed. Most of the corps members were given prescription list to get the drugs at designated pharmacies at the mammy market. On the last day of the week, Efemena said goodbye to her crew and some new friends she had made, packed her small bag and was dropped off at the park by the studio manager.

When she got home, Efemena took some pain relievers and slept. She woke up at night feeling nauseated; the tea and bread she ate for dinner were all emptied in the toilet bowl. Back in the bedroom she was getting scared. She picked up the phone to call her mother and tell her her health condition but decided to call her in the morning. Efemena moved around her room thinking.

"Oh no! It can't be, I cannot be, I'm not, am I?" she thought in shock.

She had gone far from her district to have the test done; doing it within her neighbourhood would have created suspicion. It was positive, she was five weeks gone, the thought of conceiving had not crossed her mind, why would she not be pregnant when it had escaped her mind to buy contraceptive pills on the day she had sex with Jamuike? There had been sanitation and all the shops were locked. She had also made him drive at night to avoid being seen.

After the test, Efemena had booked an appointment with the pharmacist for termination the day after tomorrow. She could not have this baby, it would affect a lot of plans and goals, her personal life and career would become stagnant. She placed her palm on her tummy and spoke to the embryo forming within.

"I am so sorry, my unborn baby, please you have to pardon your poor mummy, your birth would shatter my goals and make me a disappointment to my parents and a disgrace to my family's name. I intend to go places, having you at this time and out of wedlock will cut my wings to fly, please, my child, please, forgive me for I am about to offend you and God's will."

She would have continued her pleas, but there was a loud bang at the door and an angry male voice shouted. "Efemena! Mena! Mena! Open this damn door right now!"

"That's Jamuike," she muttered to herself. "What could he be doing at my house?"

He didn't give her time to fathom why as he continually banged the door.

As she walked towards the door, she shouted. "Hold on I will open before you break my door."

The moment she opened, Jamuike barged in pointing a finger at her. "Don't you dare kill my child, you hear me?"

"How do you mean, do you see your baby drowning in my house, do you even have a child?"

"Don't play dumb with me, Efemena, that pharmacist you booked a murder appointment with is my cousin!" Jamuike barked at her.

"That's not true, Ike." Efemena was shocked.

"Oh, it is just too true, my lady. I visited him at his office and he told me about your secret mission."

"But how, he does not even know me, how did he get to know you might be the father of this child?"

"Who does not know Efemena in this town, the entrepreneur?"

"That does not explain why he thought you should be the father of my child."

"Well I told him of our romantic escapade."

"What! How dare you?"

"That's not the issue here; the point is that no harm comes to my unborn child."

Efemena shook her head, "I cannot keep this pregnancy. Jamuike, I cannot."

"I am sorry, honey, you would have to, you are the first lady to ever conceive for me to the best of my knowledge and I am not going to let you make me childless."

"Jamuike, please, don't do this to me, you can have as many ladies who can have dozens of kids for you but right now, I cannot have this baby. I need to go home after my service here. I have told you some of my dreams, for whatever reason I don't want to stay back in this town." Efemena was at the brink of tears.

"If you step your feet into that pharmacy again or any other hospital, I assure you, Mena, that priced discharge certificate you seek would be terminated."

Efemena screamed. "Jamuike!"

"Yes, I would charge you to court. It is a good thing you serve in the local government. Emeka saw you naked in my bedroom and my cousin diagnosed you to be pregnant."

"But I was not naked. I was half naked!" Efemena yelled justifying herself.

"What difference does that make? Go mad if you must, but keep my baby sane. Congratulations, Mena," he said to her without smiling and stormed out. She slumped into the chair in her living room. In running away from her shadows, she had exposed herself on a stage and plunged into a frightening crowd. How could fate be so crazily twisted?

"O fate, how unfair you are to me, my whole dream is going to crumble, shattering into pieces all because of one night of intoxicated sex that I was not even conscious of."

Efemena cried and her eyes became sullen. She cried for herself, her future, family's reaction, pleading with destiny to reverse itself. She crawled into bed and allowed the tears soak her pillow.

She wiped her face with her gown when she heard the sound of sirens. She looked out from her window and saw some policemen entering the compound. They advanced towards Dennis' door. Efemena hurriedly dropped a shawl over her armless gown as she heard Dennis shouting, *"Oga officer, take am easy nau, wetin I do, wetin I do? See as you dey rough handle me like say I kill person. I'm not a criminal o."*

"Will you shut up and move! You are worse than a criminal." The officer shoved him towards the gate.

"Pastor, is he the one?" the policeman asked the clergy she had seen in Dennis' room.

"Yes, that is the son of the devil that has been molesting little boys in Sunday school. Officers, lock him up. He deserves to rot in jail."

Dennis was shocked and shouted "Pastor! It's me Dennis, your boy."

"Will you shut up! You spawn of the devil. Officers, take him before he corrupts all the boys in the neighbourhood, only God knows how many little boys he has initiated into homosexuality." The pastor made the sign of the cross as they dragged Dennis and heaved him into the waiting patrol van.

Efemena walked like she was in a trance back to her house. She understood the whole picture of what had just transpired. That night, she cried all the tears in her heart, for Dennis and herself. The poor boy had been betrayed by his lover.

The following afternoon, Efemena visited Dennis at the police station. He confirmed what she suspected. The pastor sold him out since someone caught them in the act. "Before the intruder would spill the beans, he went against me because I refused to tell him who saw us."

She asked him if she was in any danger. He assured her that the pastor did not see her face and warned Efemena to never speak about it. "The pastor is a dangerous breed, a wolf that parades in sheep's clothing."

Dennis had been exposed; definitely he would be prosecuted and sentenced to serve the required jail term for his crime. He was not guilty of the little boys, he never engaged anyone below thirty. Efemena was dumbfounded; she said goodbye and left the station. The image of Dennis' body and sad look haunted her all the way home.

The sad day had not ended for Efemena. She saw Antonia running towards the bus stop, her slippers in hand. Antonia flagged Efemena who stamped on the brake. She got out of the car and ran to the distressed girl who ran to meet her. She had worry and fear all over her face and her hands were trembling.

"Mena, please come and help."

"Come, get into the car," Efemena urged her.

Antonia refused and ran back towards their compound. Efemena entered her car and drove to the compound. The girls were already outside the gate. Ada was covered in blood; her eyes were tightly closed as she groaned in pains.

"Oh my God! What happened? Bring her in; quickly, put her in the back seat."

Antonia got into the passenger's seat, crying and praying. Efemena tried not to look at the sight on the back seat. She needed to focus on the road and get to the hospital safely because the sight might destabilize her.

She was out of danger and her womb cleansed. Ada took overdose of labour inducement pills to abort the foetus in her womb. She laid on the bed crying softly.

"Ada, please stop crying, you should be thanking God you are fine," Efemena gently rubbed her palm.

"I didn't want that baby. Thanks for saving my life though. But nothing would have stopped me from getting rid of it. I could not keep it."

Efemena heard her own words, *I cannot keep this baby,* and realized she did not have any moral justification. Still she consoled the distraught girl, her case was severe because the pregnancy was past the first trimester and aborting at that stage was dangerous. She could have died.

"Don't talk that way, Ada. That was dangerous."

"Efemena, stop, I cannot keep it, I will rather die, let me die instead. What will I be living for? A fool like me does not deserve to constitute nuisance to my peers and family. I've been a fool." She wept bitterly.

"Shhh! You are not a fool, neither are you a nuisance to anybody. You will be a successful graduate and a proud mother someday."

"Babe, you have no idea of what I have been through. I am not a student. I was on probation in my first year, and in the second year, my CGPA was nothing." She sobbed.

"It is okay; we should not be talking about this now. You still have your future ahead, brighter days await you. If you will just live, and be positive. Stop crying, my dear. I'm pregnant too and do not want to keep the child. I am being forced by the father to keep it against my wish."

"Well, at least the father wants the baby; my story is different and worse. I have dated that man for two years and I have had eight abortions, and now this." She wept bitterly as she looked down at her scarred stomach.

Efemena refrained herself from screaming aloud.

"My story is so pathetic. I had decided this time I was not getting rid of this like he always told me to. I would keep it, I told myself 'it was high time we got married'. He had postponed our getting married for too long. Last week when I travelled to his permanent residence in Abang, I met his beautiful wife, and five beautiful children; three boys and two girls. He introduced me as his colleague's girlfriend who was always coming to him anytime I had challenges in my relationship. Efemena, the woman was so kind to me, she allowed me to stay in her home for two days, and took care of me."

"Did she?"

"Yes. My conscience did not allow me say a word that will hurt her family. I hid my hurt and the betrayal and on the third day, I left their home. I went to his office on Monday because it all felt like a dream. I wanted to be sure of what I had seen. Efemena, that guy is a slimy bastard."

"I am so sorry you had this unfortunate encounter with him."

Tears gathered in Ada's eyes. "How this fool can live amongst sensible people eludes me. I cannot bear it. I would rather die and relieve the world of my stupidity. His workplace is here, and I was just the side whore he kept in his apartment." Ada wept profusely.

"Promise me you won't try this again. I will ensure you get back to school, and will support you."

Ada opened her eyes. "Really, you will do that for me, babe?"

"Yes and more; if you fight these negative emotions."

Ada made an effort to stand up but Efemena held her shoulders and carefully laid her back.

"Thank you so much, Mena, I owe you my life. God bless you. Thank you so much."

"You are welcome, dear. We thank our faithful God for all the possibilities. Now smile." Ada smiled.

Efemena picked the flask Antonia brought an hour ago from the floor and served the hot pepper soup. Ada stared at the soup as Efemena made plans in her head. She thought of making Ada her maid of honour. That evening, Efemena took a long walk. The small market peered at her like a child carried away with playing by the river. Efemena passed the boundary that divided the street of her neighbourhood onto the main road. As she crossed; the rains poured torrentially on the earth. Efemena looked up to the sky and felt the harsh beat of the liquids on her face. In a far distance, some dogs barked ferociously and goats bleated in their tethers.

Two weeks later, Efemena and Jamuike got married. It was a small reception with few guests at the local government. They had a court wedding. Efemena could not afford losing her certificate. Jamuike could not have an illegitimate child; his custom demanded that he married the mother of his child. They had settled on the baby bond relationship. Efemena's father was furious with her and dammed his duty to give her out in marriage; he warned her mother not to attend the wedding. It was her brother who stood as witness and her only family in attendance.

Jamuike as a son of the soil had more relations who made it memorable for him. His parents, siblings and relatives were joyous and expectant of a newborn. Some of Efemena's colleagues at the local government made it to the reception; they tried to make her smile and dance. Efemena had a lot on her mind. She was sad she was quitting spinsterhood accidentally; envious of the single ladies who flirted with their dance partners with ease. She could not wait for this day to be over; her eyes roamed and found Jamuike greeting guests. He looked handsome in his tuxedo.

"Oh, Jamuike, just look at you, it is more potent to betray a love affair than tarnish true friendship. You were my friend and yet you have proudly crushed my happiness," Efemena mused.

Her supervisor, Mrs Comfort Nwabueze, noticed the sullen mood and came around to hug her.

"Mena, my girl, why this awful look? It is not nice for this day. Come on, cheer up." Mrs Comfort touched her chin.

"Ma'am, you know this is not a happy celebration for me. If I had my way, I would put on a black dress and mourn my fate."

She had told her what happened between her and Jamuike a week before now, she needed someone to talk to about the circumstances engineering their union and she found an empathetic confidante in Mrs Comfort.

"Efemena, I believe everything will work out for good, in time you will find love with your husband. Jamuike is not such a bad chap, my dear."

"I don't like it here, the last thing on my mind was to settle down here." Efemena lamented.

"Really, but you have always been happy here, have you been pretending?" Mrs Comfort asked.

"No, Ma'am. I make the most of every moment to be happy in any place I find myself, but there is a big difference now. Just like when I was at camp, I endured because in a few weeks I was getting out. Same applies to the fact I have some months left before I leave. But I am stuck where I am."

Mrs Comfort touched Efemena tenderly on her right cheek. She lacked the words to console the unhappy bride.

❦ *Fifteen* ❦

Efemena's new status did not deter her from normal activities. The differences were a slight increase in her body size, fatigue, nausea and spitting. She held herself back from scratching her body. Her mother told her it would help keep off stretch marks on her stomach during and after pregnancy. She moved to her husband's apartment, left her house open for corps members who needed temporary shelter.

They lived as estranged couples. Barely saying five sentences to each other in a week, took their separate cars to work, but ate from same pot. Efemena prepared the meals whether money came from her or Jamuike's wallet.

She did only her laundry and slept in a separate room. Efemena saw no reason to put any effort into the sham of a marriage and seized every opportunity to stay at work, CDS meeting and hospital for check-ups.

Jamuike was irritated by her attitude, and he rebuked her one night. "Efemena, where are you coming from at this hour?"

She looked at her wristwatch. "Jamuike, it is just 9:45 pm," she said.

"Yea, it is inappropriate for a married woman to be arriving home at this time."

"Says who, Mr Time Keeper? Please excuse me, I am too tired. I need rest."

"Efemena, this nonsense of yours has to stop. I won't have you make people call me a weakling who cannot call his wife to order."

"Oh you mean you haven't noticed the neighbours gossiping about our loveless marriage? Get ready for more, my darling hubby."

"Efemena, please we can make this work, we can build love, baby."

"Is that so? Anyway, there has never been love. You disregarded my love when you maliciously took me to wife. If there was ever one from me, it is now in rubbles. Forget it. Now, husband, if you will excuse me I need to have my bath and sleep."

"Your mother called. Your number was not reachable."

"I will call her up in the morning. I hope it's not a crucial matter, I could call now." She took her phone to dial her mother's number.

"Never mind, she dropped a message for you. I can see you have plantains in your shopping bag, but you should not eat them."

"Why is that?" She raised her eyebrows.

"She said you should avoid it during pregnancy. If you eat plantains, there would be crack on the baby's head or a dividing line at the centre of his or her head."

Efemena smirked. "Ike, are you sure you have not added salt and maggi to what she said? I mean that is so weird." She rolled her eyeballs.

"Do it anyway, your mother said so. You should know better than ignoring cultural beliefs. You may not fancy superstitions but, Madam, do as your mother has said. Call her to verify tomorrow."

"Okay I will." Efemena walked into the kitchen to drop the shopping bag on the kitchen slab. She turned to go to her room when Jamuike spoke.

"The landlord brought a formal notice for us to evacuate this apartment, as you know it is only rented to bachelors. He gave us the grace of two weeks as a wedding present. I have been searching for another place. I was thinking maybe we could put up at your place until I get a decent home."

"We cannot go to my apartment. I have seen a house up for lease, few miles from the local government secretariat."

"Okay nice, how is it?"

"It's a four-bedroom apartment and looks gorgeous."

"Good, we can check it out tomorrow. We will ride in my car. Thanks and good night," he replied curtly.

"You are welcome, good night."

Efemena went to her room. Jamuike exercised his knuckles by mildly pressing each finger down. He thought about tomorrow's movement and how it would go. He needed to move his family out to avoid embarrassment. The landlord was on his neck and his loveless wife was not cooperating. Efemena's words sank heavily in his heart.

The house was gorgeous as Efemena had said, it was the perfect home, nevertheless Jamuike said he could not afford the amount, there was no way he could pay two years upfront. He was a civil servant; he could not pay for it, especially with a baby on the way, he would have more responsibilities. Efemena wanted it; a beautiful house with balcony and swimming pool. A busy town could add colours to her mood. Without many objections, Jamuike gratefully conceded they shared the bill. Arrangements were made and the bills paid. In less than a week they moved in.

They settled in their new house with their old attitude, they had more space to live as flat mates. As her stomach grew, she became easily tired. She went shopping, bought washing machine, split air conditioner, juice extractor and jogging kits. Efemena got home with a permanent marker and wrote her maiden name 'Efemena Aruegodore' on every item. Jamuike stared in awe. He did not say a word, he just followed her moves with raised eyebrow. Everything went by so fast within the space of four weeks.

Today marked the third week and final day of orientation of the batch C. The batch of corps members posted to the community would be escorted by existing corps members who had gone very early in the morning to bring them to the *corpers* lodge. At last they arrived; they were welcomed at the *corpers* lodge. They were immediately given a long list of rules and regulations and assigned to rooms in the house. All the vice presidents of the various CDS groups – Social, Mass Literacy, Publicity, Millennium Development Goals, The Nigerian Red Cross, Gender Vanguard, Service Compact, HIV-PET, Federal Road Safety Corp Club, and Freedom of Information Act – were assigned to cook for three days at the *corpers* lodge It was a fine Thursday, every POP ceremony of the NYSC was always carried out on Thursday.

At 10 am, Efemena strolled down to the lodge where cooking was ongoing at the outer kitchen. It was a warm community of domestic belles, happy to be playing mother hens to their chicks just hatched from camp. The menu was: *egusi* soup with *Eba* on the evening of their arrival, rice and stew in the morning, beans in the evening, *jollof rice* for the last day.

The meals were a replica of the camp format, but the meat this time was cut into bigger pieces unlike the gravel sized beef then. The *egusi* soup was thick and sumptuous, spiced and garnished with enough crayfish, vegetables, dried and stock fishes. While the soup was steaming, some of the males were called to make the *Eba*. It was one expert among them that moulded the *garri*, that no powder was left untouched with hot water, and it was almost perfect.

They were addressed by the commander who assured them that the lives of corps members were worth more than gold and it was their priority to protect them, but first they must assist them by being conscious and vigilant of their surroundings. The commander congratulated them on a successful orientation at camp. He also bought airtime vouchers of their preferred networks, one hundred naira (₦100) worth each.

Meanwhile the food had been brought in. This time no meal ticket was required, the instruction was for them all to queue with their eating utensils. They were satisfied because the food served was richer than what they were used to in the past weeks. Efemena and her batch members were glad with the nice comments on the meat size and rich soup. They felt fulfilled, because their culinary goal was to deviate from past norms of preparing watery soup with tiny meat.

Because of her delicate condition, Efemena was permitted to go home and rest. On her way home, she witnessed an interesting show. There was a ruckus at an army checkpoint. She stopped an ice cream peddler to find out what triggered the teeming crowd. Her interest was heightened when she sighted a female corps member in the gathering.

By the ice cream seller's narration, the lady when boarding the tricycle, told the driver she only had thirty naira (₦30) for fare. That was the usual fee, except for greedy drivers, who charged fifty naira. At her stop, she paid him, but the driver held her Khaki jacket. He insisted he never agreed for the lesser fee, that she must pay up. He waved off intrusions from passengers in the same vehicle. A reverend sister said he had agreed. Still, he did not let her go, pressing for twenty naira balance. He heedlessly paid no attention to anybody's plea. His angels were probably observing siesta as some soldiers met him there. He was asked to sit in a dirty pool of water, roll thirty times on the ground, and make frog jump movements twenty times. He was given water and detergent to wash their patrol van because he had assaulted a paramilitary.

For a while now, Efemena had lost her sense of humour. She wore a big smile and laughed the rest of her way home. Some measure of respect and protection came with the status of a serving corps member. Khaki was highly regarded irrespective of body size, big or small; a federal government charge is not one to fiddle with.

✳　　✳　　✳　　✳　　✳

Mariam came into the passage and dragged herself to the living room; She was tightening the straps of her brassiere when her mum saw her.

"Where are you coming from, Madam? I have been calling your name for the past five minutes, and you felt too big to answer. I guess your ears have become deaf that you no longer hearken to my calls,right?"

"Sorry, Mama, I was just having a quick nap in my room," she replied.

"Napping, at this time? Mariam, it is barely past 10 am, and you are back to sleep, what time did you wake up? Besides, where did you sleep because I was in your room?"

"Oh, Mama, I forgot, Daddy asked me to bring my admission letter."

Mrs Bello was confused. "From napping, to tendering admission letter. Mariam, I hope you have not started sleepwalking? Anyway, that is okay, go now to the kitchen and unpack the items I bought. We need to start preparing the meals, there is no food left in the freezer."

"Okay, Mama." She walked into the kitchen and did as instructed.

Some minutes later, her mum joined her and they prepared food. They heard a knock, "Mrs Bello?"

"Yeah. Mariam, wash the oil on your fingers and check who is at the door."

"Okay Mama." she wiped her hands with a napkin.

"I hope you shook the oil well; I do not want a part thick and the other light."

"Yes, Mama, I shook it well."

"Okay, go quick."

Mariam rushed to the door. She came in with Efemena.

"Mama Mariam, sorry for bothering you, Ma'am."

"It is okay, Mama Twins." Efemena laughed at Mrs Bello's statement, rubbing her belly.

"Who said it is a twin, Mama Mariam? You have started. If it happens that way, I will give you one and keep the other."

"I am ready. There are lots of food in this home. She would have siblings to play with." They both laughed, while Mariam smiled warily.

"I hear, no wahala be that."

"Ah at all. So, what brings you, Mama Twins?"

"I came to ask for your grinding stone."

"Okay, I just used it. Hope you would not mind, I ground *dawadawa* on it."

"Not at all. It's also what I want to grind, it will make my food even tastier." They laughed.

"Oh good, there it is." Efemena moved to carry it, but Mrs Bello stopped her.

"Aha...aha...aha...it is too heavy for you, Mama Twins."

"I can carry it, Ma."

"Ehen, not while Mariam is here. Mariam, take it to your aunt's flat."

"Okay, Mama." She lifted the grinding stone and made for Efemena's house.

"Thank you, Ma, I will return it as soon as I am done. Thank you Mariam"

"You are welcome, Auntie." Efemena opened the kitchen door for Mariam and they both left while Mrs Bello continued her cooking.

At dinner in Mr Bello's house, he began the discussion on Mariam's preparation for the university. He picked a glass of water, drank out of it and placed it back on the table.

"Mariam?" he called and cleared his throat.

"Yes, Baba," she looked up from her meal.

"Do you prefer to live in the school hostel, or to stay back and go to school from home?" He fixed a smug stare on Mariam, while her eyes remained nervously on her food.

"Mariam, your father has just asked you a question," Mrs Bello said to her.

"Hmm, Baba, I want to stay off-campus, get my own apartment." She quickly pleaded when she noticed the displeasure on her father's face. "Please, Baba."

"No, young lady. You will not live outside the school premises. If you are not going to stay at home, then hostel accommodation is your only choice," he replied in a stern voice.

"No, please, Baba. I don't want to stay in an unkempt environment. The school hostels are unhealthy, Baba."

"Your studies should be your priority; you can always leave the discomfort of a hostel and study in the serenity of a library, and also, keep the confines of your room neat."

Mariam began to grumble; her face tightened in disagreement. "Oh I see, I get it now, you want to camp your boyfriend in your room right? You want an avenue where men can visit you at will." Mariam and her mother were shocked to hear his outburst.

Mrs Bello responded, "Aha, my dear, haba. You should not talk or think that way of your daughter, seeing her in such manner is not fair at all. I am supporting her on this, whether she accommodates a boyfriend or not, I believe she is old enough to make wise decisions for herself."

"Would you allow me speak to our child, woman? I am concerned about her welfare."

"You mean to say you are disturbed about her existing or intended sex life? That's inevitable, Isiaka. If you are so worried, then you should deprive her of a university education then. Why are you not bothered about lecturers subjecting students to sexual harassment on the issues of sex for marks? Why don't you send your daughter to western universities so you are assured no lecturer would approach her for sex?"

"That's the last thing I would do. She would remain at home and school as long as I am her sponsor because I am not a

130

stealing politician. I see you want to play dumb that you are not aware that the FG has restricted credit card use abroad. Do I sense a plan to make me go bankrupt here? Anyway, I insist she wants to stay out so she can entertain boys in her apartment." He swallowed his wheat balls.

"Bello, remember this is not her first attempt at seeking for admission. It is her fourth time of writing JAMB and post-UTME. Thanks to the good Lord we serve and her tenacity, she is an undergraduate with a promising future. I don't think she would want to squash this opportunity. It is wrong for you to cook up those negative thoughts. Please, let her stay off-campus if it is her wish, most school hostels can be horrible indeed. Think of the influence of peer groups into sexual acts, cultism, and not to mention toilet infections or food poisoning because they have to improvise a cooking area at their bed corners. What are we saying: with the proximity of fire, the room may be gutted in flames, the prospects are galling! God forbid! And that news about the cleaners rummaging through the dumpsites at the back of girls' hostels frightens me. An old woman was caught with about two hundred wraps of used sanitary towels; goodness knows what she wants with them, and what she has done with previous pads."

"Let her speak, woman, she has a tongue doesn't she?" Mrs Bello eyed her husband coldly, and picked at her food. "Mariam, is that what you really want, to live away from home and campus lodging?"

"Yes, Baba, I want to live off-campus."

"Okay as you wish, we will begin arrangement for that as soon as possible," he spoke in a dry tone, and left the dining with an expressionless face.

Mrs Bello placed her hand on Mariam's. "That is okay, Mariam. I am assuring you everything will be fine, your wish shall be fulfilled, my daughter. Eat your meal, my dear." Mariam nodded her head and picked fish from the soup.

"Hmmm. Mama, why is Baba vehemently opposed to Mariam

staying off-campus? He did not object when Juliana gained admission. She is even four years younger than Mariam." Danladi laughed and continued, "Mummy, your husband can be so unpredictable and funny sometimes eh."

"Will you shush your mouth, you silly young man! Either I or your father should never hear such words from you again, do I make myself clear?"

"Yeah."

"Good, now keep quiet, let us conclude our meal in peace." Danladi closed his mouth as he was about to say something. "Come, cheer up, my baby. You want to be fast about eating your food else you miss out on the shopping I have planned, we will get some new clothes and other provisions."

Mariam hurriedly snapped out of her sour mood. "Mama!"

"Yeah, for you and you alone, dear."

"Oh, Mama. Thank you so much." She covered her mouth. "God bless you, Mama, I didn't see that coming at all, just last week we went shopping, Mama, and yet again."

"And we will go for another; again and again. You are welcome, Mariam, nothing is too much for any of my children as long as I and your father are alive, our resources are capable. All we pray is for long life and prosperity."

"Yes, yes, Mama. Amen and amen," Mariam sang. They resumed eating and the atmosphere became cheerful.

Later in the night, Mariam whispered in her room as she made a call. "That decision was a special consideration for our own good. It will afford us more privacy and time, baby." She paused to listen to the voice on the other side.

"I'm happy you now agree with me, together we'll have lots of fun in my own apartment. Honey, I hope you will help to pick some items for the room; we need to give it a very fine look. We should go for pink and white colours." She waited for the other person to speak.

"Hey look, boo, we will be sharing this room together does not mean it'll be our room. It's mine, and mine alone, you're only welcome as a loveable guest." She giggled excitedly.

"We can't have anything masculine in view, boo, it's my room, and mine alone please." Mariam paused to listen to the voice on the phone.

"But of course I'm old enough to have a boyfriend, still it doesn't mean I've to flaunt it for all to see, also someone acted as though it was forbidden to have a boyfriend."

Again she paused to listen, then laughed. "You're asking me who as if you do not know. Goodnight. I'm feeling so sleepy." She waited for a response from the receiver and then ended the call.

"Oh, I cannot wait to begin school, and of course be at ease with my baby." She blushed, summersaulted lightly on her bed, put out the light and tucked herself in. The room was hot but for the mosquitoes buzzing around to suck her blood at any opportunity, the cover was needful.

Ada was sitting in a restaurant, eating, when she noticed a young man walk towards her.

"Hi, gorgeous."

"Hello, manly," she appraised him and then spotted his shiny wedding band. "He is even newly married. Lord, please conceal my face from these adulterous men. Let me be invisible to their lustful eyes; at least this one is sincere by leaving his ring on," she thought to herself.

"My name is …" Ada interrupted him before he said his name.

"W.O.M.A.N.I.Z.E.R," she said the letters one after the other and pronounced it womanizer."

"Excuse me, I beg your pardon, you must be mistaken."

"Nope, I cannot be mistaken; it's so obvious that's what you are."

"That's not right, I'll clear this misunderstanding. My name is Wo …"

"Save it. Just shove your name down your throat."

"Okay, can I have a seat at least? I must confess I'm falling for you. I love you."

Ada looked at him from his head to toe rudely. "You can sit, but not at this table. And before you defend yourself by saying this is a public restaurant and you can sit anywhere you please, respect yourself and get your hitched ass *outta* my face."

"Hold on baby, you're being too harsh on a gentleman."

"Now I'm irritated. Will you leave my presence before I puke some nonsense on your gentle jerk foolery?"

"Baby"

She bent to remove a pair of her shoe. "You just call me baby one more time, dog."

"Damn! You're just an old ass bitch; no responsible man will approach you, no wonder you're tired and single."

"Thanks Mr Responsible. I just pity your unlucky wife at home. Get lost! I'll rather remain single than to be associated with an uncircumcised pig." She stuck her tongue out. She picked her cutleries to eat but she had already lost appetite. She left the restaurant.

Ada narrated her encounter with a certain man at the restaurant to Efemena. "Just tell me when you are done laughing, so I can continue with my pitiable story." She propped her face on her chin and watched Efemena laughing.

"It's not that I'm laughing."

"Oh, oh, so tell me, my dearest friend, what are you doing if not making a big joke out of this pathetic situation?"

"Please do not mind me; don't take me serious, I can't just help it." She continued laughing hysterically.

Ada hissed and stood up. "Let me entertain myself while you are at this. What did you cook?"

Ada made her way to the kitchen. Some minutes later, she came out with a tray of soup and eba. She sat and smiled satisfactorily.

"This is one good thing about a married woman's house; you find sumptuous and delicious meals. This soup is deliciously epic."

"You have made yourself at home in my kitchen?"

"Why not, was I not your maid of honour? I served a great role in your marriage when I held your gown and walked the aisle behind you." She grinned.

Efemena laughed. "You are so funny, I hope you have not emptied the pot of meat, my husband is yet to eat."

"You know as much as I know, that the meat and fish in that pot can feed an army, so let me have a nice meal, okay? Please, Madam."

"Like my chastisement has stopped you from eating your meal, *abeg carry go joor.* Ada, some men are really mean, they can easily fool ladies without their wedding band on, just like James."

"You can say that again my dear friend. That dude is worse than the serpent in the garden of Eden."

"So what do you intend to do now?"

"For now, it's a no-no for me in relationships. I'll never say yes to any man until the grand finale, at the altar."

"Ada, should that be the criteria really? Is that approach wise, babe, what if he's marrying you as a second wife?"

"At this point in life, my dear I do not mind, so long he is marrying me, I do not care if he is married to fifty women. With his many wives and concubines, King Solomon was still loved by God and was a very fortunate man."

"Wait a minute! Just hold on, do not tell me your mentality has deteriorated so low."

"There, gotcha! I was kidding, dear; you know I would never descend so low. I pray to God every day for a monogamous union, it makes matrimony holy, at least God has saved this one girl from delving into polygamy. You know when I was pregnant, nothing could have stopped me from making that man marry me, and at all cost. I would neither have aborted, nor had it out of wedlock, but for the ugly event. The wife was too nice. I was shattered."

"That's okay, that reality would have been scary; I shudder at the uncomfortable life you would have lived."

"Mena, what do you think of a man with excess pride?"

"Not good enough. Why do you ask, Ada?"

"And ego that's uncalled for?"

"It's not good enough for any human. Such a man will make you feel small. You might not be happy, Ada."

"I am mostly attracted to proud men. I feel there is this aura to the utter ego they exude. I have told myself to overlook that, but, Mena, why is it that humble, honest guys don't find me good enough? Why do I always have to end up with the cunning, lying and cheating men?"

"We all ask ourselves that, Ada. Someone who loves themselves too much cannot find space to love you enough. It is not as if we all don't have pride, but when it's not in check, so many things can go wrong."

"My fantasy as a girl was to have my prince charming all to myself. I never dreamt of dating or had the slightest thought of getting involved with a married man. Why am I so unlucky?"

"A lot of women never dreamt of dating married men, but women are attracted to the genes of successful men; and some of such guys manipulate desperate women, taking advantage of their weakness of financial insecurities or lack of emotional relations."

They were both silent when Efemena heard the sound of Jamuike's car.

"Jamuike is home. You look so sullen, cheer up, Ada, all will be well okay, cheer up girl."

"Oh great, glad I will see him before I leave. God knows when next I will visit your house, probably for the naming ceremony of my goddaughter." Ada smiled.

"You this girl eh, and what makes you think it is a female child?"

"I do not know, but just give me a goddaughter. Since as your maid of honour, I am the first girl of my parents, destiny is likely to give you a female child first."

Efemena threw a pillow at Ada; laughing and shaking her head at her friend's statement. "You are one naughty girl I have met in this world," she drawled as they heard footsteps at the door.

"That must be Jamuike, come on, wife, go and get the door." Ada winked at her. She stuck her tongue out at Ada, smoothened the creases on her dress as she opened the door.

"Welcome," she reluctantly received her husband's kiss, and pecked him on the cheek too. Efemena noticed Ifeoma and blushed. "Welcome, sister-in-law. Jamuike did not tell me he would bring you himself. I have been expecting you long before now. How was your trip?"

"Thanks, my wife. It was a smooth flight. He virtually picked me right from air. Sorry for coming late, I hope you have not served my meal." Ifeoma joked and they all laughed.

Efemena unconsciously remained at the entrance, preventing Ifeoma and Jamuike from gaining access. "Baby, if you don't mind, can you just move aside so we may come in?" Jamuike gestured to Efemena to move aside with his left hand.

"Oh! Sorry, Ike, please come in. Ifeoma, please I am sorry."

"Definitely, you got carried away with your husband's presence. Love is indeed sweet, and marriage even sweeter! I will get in now. You can continue to hug each other. Please, excuse me." They laughed as they entered. Efemena quickly served their meal and invited her in-law to the table.

"I have been dreaming of your pot of soup from the airport." Ifeoma exhaled the aroma in the living room. "I could not wait to have a taste of your food again."

"And I have missed eating my friend's delicacies for a long while."

"Ada! You are a glutton. You just ate like an hour ago."

"I can't get enough of your meal. Oh, you thought by referring to me as a glutton in front of Jamuike and Ifeoma, I will be embarrassed? Well sorry to burst your bubble, girl, please serve my meal." They laughed and ate in silence. Ada left an hour after. After the meal, Efemena started a jovial discussion about the epileptic power supply in their neighbourhood and the growing cost of living.

✡ ✡ ✡ ✡ ✡

Jamuike and Efemena were still in bed. He rubbed his chest feeling satiated. He was impressed with Efemena's devotion because of his sister's presence. Their act was being well played. They agreed to appear like a loving couple to Ifeoma. Jamuike requested that from Efemena so that his sister would not have the wrong idea of his marriage, he had pleaded. Efemena readily agreed because she needed to satisfy her sexual cravings in bed.

"You will get over the coldness very soon, baby, because there are many erotic ways I want to teach you how to love. I would want us to explore sensually, Jamuike said and got off the bed."

"I will clean up; go through the newspaper and my mails. See that breakfast is ready soon, babe."

Efemena did not respond. She slept like a statue. He knew she was awake. He smiled and dropped light pecks on her cheeks. Jamuike headed to the bathroom.

At the sound of the door, Efemena hurriedly got off bed. She smiled satisfactorily. She was excited this morning. She began tidying up the house, humming as she worked.

"Efemena, go get breakfast ready, I am hungry. Ifeoma would be hungry too and she might still be hesitant to make herself comfortable in your kitchen."

"Yes, right away, you are right, Jamuike."

"Thank you, you are radiant this morning." She blushed. Efemena walked out so fast like she would melt the next minute.

"Aha! What is this coyness?" Jamuike asked loudly. He presumed it was one of her pregnancy mood swings. Whatever the reason, he was happy with the new atmosphere of their marriage, maybe things will stay this way after Ifeoma leaves the house. Jamuike prayed it should be as he was pleased with this new turn. This part of Efemena was appealing. He wondered if Ifeoma had discussed with her; maybe Ifeoma had noticed the void in his marriage. Jamuike shook his head; it was possible because his sister was very sensitive.

He shouted to his wife's retreating figure. "I love you, baby, even if you do not say it, I know you do, and I can't wait for you to say it lovingly, my heart yearns for those words."

Efemena smiled while Jamuike resignedly went into the bath, unaware of the impact of his words on Efemena. Jamuike entered the kitchen and tenderly held Efemena by her shoulder. He would have loved to wrap his arms around her baby bump, but he was unsure of Efemena's reaction.

"It's beautiful being married, and it is possible because I married an angel. I love you."

Efemena carefully covered the flask she just poured water into and faced Jamuike. "Hmmm. I love you, too."

"Ah. You fill my heart with bubbles this morning. What took you so long to say those lovable words? I have waited to hear it but it seemed it was going to take forever before you utter them. I love you so much, baby."

Efemena grinned widely. "I was just joking. I wanted to hear how saying 'I love you' would sound, Ike." She took sliced bread from the fridge and smiled.

"Ah, ah, not again. Come on, Mena, we can make it work. Let love happen. I know you love me as much as I do, and one day you will admit it sincerely."

"Stop being arrogant, Ike. We are only permitted till Ifeoma leaves. We are also free to play, it heightens our passion for some night activities."

"Come on, let me help you with that." Jamuike carried the breakfast tray.

"Thanks, that's so thoughtful of you."

"Anything for you." He wink.

Sixteen

The arrival of the batch **C** corps members marked less than one month to Efemena's passing out parade, a period she would have gladly looked forward to to return home. She would stay back in this town; not her own wish but for her careless disposition. Her beloved father wanted nothing with her. Each stage of her pregnancy, she communicated with her mother through phone calls and texts.

"I put all the blame on myself and nobody else, it is my cross I am carrying. But please, my God, do not nail me so hard to the strong pillar of sadness and uncertainty." As she soliloquized, soft raps came on the front door, someone was knocking.

"Who is it?" Efemena shouted.

"It is your wildest imagination. The unexpected and you must pay my money or else the whole neighbourhood will know your true colour today," a male voice replied.

"What in the world are you talking about?" Efemena was curious to know who the clown was. She walked toward the door ready to scold whoever it was.

"Surprise! Hey, hey, Efemena, how are you doing gorgeous mama to be?" Osaze shouted.

Efemena laughed and placed her hand on her stomach. "Osaze! You clown, my instinct told me it was you, but I didn't want to believe because I did not give you the directions to my house plus that change in your tone. Come in, you are welcome to my home."

Osaze strolled in surveying the house. "You've got a beautiful place here,Efemena, homely mama; motherhood will suit you. Hmmm, but why didn't you chill for us to get married, instead you hurriedly got hitched to Mr charming clerk, when you decisively told me you were not going to walk down the aisle until hundred years to come," he teased.

She laughed. "That's a lie, Osaze. I never uttered that bizarre statement and you know it. Take a seat please, but mind you, I don't have a bar corner in my house so you just have to settle for juice."

"Hey, Mena, you know I don't like soft drinks, too sugary for my taste. I'm a man and soon I will be scoring goals like your hubby."

"Good for you, much intake of sugar kills the sperm potency of a man. So that's why you spend half of your allowance on beer and nkwobi before marriage eh?"

"Efemena, you are there! But you forgot to add my *ofe nsala* and *abacha*."

"I know all that. Please make do with the fruit juice; you will enjoy it. Some other time, I'll buy you enough bottles."

"That's my girl talking, you're too much, if not that you are married eh, I would have showered you with hugs and pecks."

"Imagine! Not in your wildest imagination, even when I was single, you wouldn't dare."

"Yes, Ma'am. I didn't and I wouldn't now. You are a rare jewel not to be messed around with; you are too good to be toyed with."

"Thanks, Osaze, I'm lost for words to appreciate these compliments. Thank you."

"Don't mention, dear, the pleasure is mine."

There was a brief silence as Osaze drank from his glass of cold orange juice, while Efemena settled comfortably on the posh sofa. Clearing his throat, he resumed.

"Efemena, why weren't you at *CDS* meeting? I don't need to

ask if you were ill because you look radiant. Why were you absent?"

"I came in from the hospital some minutes before your arrival. I was feeling feverish this morning so I booked an appointment with my doctor, which he slated for 10 am, the same time as *CDS*. I knew I was going to be absent so I put a call to the President."

"Okay. I'm glad you are better now, but, girl, you missed out big time."

"Really? What happened, Osaze? Tell please."

"Of course, my madam. It all began on Monday."

"Monday, today is Thursday, and you are just telling me? You should have called me."

"My angel, please pardon me. I was so upset about the whole fiasco; too angry to talk about it. Now shut your pretty lips and let me talk." Efemena clamped her lips. "On Monday, the principal pasted a letter which stated that there would be curfew from 7 pm including weekends. Male and female corps members, friends; opposite sex could not visit us. Efemena, you needed to have seen us, we were as cold as ice over the preposterous rules. We were told to either give in or get out. You know we lived within the school premises."

"I was lost for words to express myself. Why would I be locked in by 7 pm? Was it my fault they were so inconsiderate to accommodate us in same quarters with their boarding students? My fellow corps members are the closest families I have in this region, you all are my brothers and sisters. If I was sick for instance and one of you came to visit, you would not be allowed to see me, according to their dictate. They also added another subject for us to teach."

"Wow, making three subjects? Are they trying to sap all your strength before the service year runs out?" Efemena was alarmed.

"And you know the instruction given by Zonal Inspector was not to teach more than two subjects. When asked to take three

142

we are to 'politely refuse'. I studied mechanical engineering. I teach Basic Science and Mathematics, plus the newly assigned Literature, a subject I did not offer in secondary school. I would need to study in order to teach, like I have nothing to do with my spare time."

"Like corps members have no life of their own aside making lesson notes and teaching in their overpopulated classrooms," Efemena hissed.

"The cheap labour we are being used for is not satisfactory, they want to enslave us. After much argument, our seniors signed under duress; they signed because they would be out in a few weeks. Greg and others chickened out because they needed clearance letter. The rest of us were asked to evacuate the school within the next forty-eight hours."

"Don't tell me you guys packed out?"

"Trust we didn't, we called the local government inspector on phone who quickly ordered the CLO to meet us at the school. The school authority was resolute: it was either we agreed to the conditions, or got lost. The annoying part was that they refused to issue us rejection letters."

"You don't mean it!" Efemena clamped her hands on her knees and sat forward in her seat with renewed interest.

"The CLO cautioned us to be calm, told us to stay back in the lodge and wait for the local government inspector who said she would come to address the issue. We stayed but were side-lined. Suddenly we ceased having power supply, the taps stopped flowing and our names were bandied about in gossip. We became refugees in our own place of primary assignment.

"It continued till Tuesday. By noon the local government inspector met with us at the *corpers* lodge. Amazingly she had changed tunes, ordered us to go back to the school, plead and get accepted or we would not do clearance. It was with great restraint we did not retaliate with a riot. I was galled by local government inspector's unemotional utterances and wondered what they must have told her.

143

"She was not helpful. So, we went down to the zonal inpector's office to report the case. He was pissed at the audacity of the school authority and the local government inspector's indifference and promised he would see that our fundamental rights were reinstated. But my dear, there was a contagious discord in the whole affair. Barely two hours after we left the zonal headquarters, he put a call through the local government inspector to the CLO to inform us to return to the school and be abiding corps members, to say sorry like loyal bingos and comport ourselves thereon.

"The proprietor of the school is an influential man of the community. The structure of the school properties hinted that but the low turnout of students and mismanagement made us doubt. The school had once bloomed with children from prestigious homes, but was shut down for years because of the high rate of kidnap that enveloped the region. The rich kids were abducted and traded for ransom. This made people withdraw their kids.

"On Wednesday morning, we were served a five count query from the state NYSC office, to be quickly filled and returned within one hour via the CLO. Efemena, you would cringe at the malicious and incriminating accusations."

"I am shivering right now. I can imagine the cold ill-treatments you guys had to go through." Efemena clasped both her kneecaps.

"Those were even the least. They alleged we smoked hard drugs, brought prostitutes into the vicinity; we fought with the teachers, came in late, we did not teach at our lecture periods but slept in our rooms during school hours."

"They are sick. What preposterous lies! These people can nail a baby to the cross." Efemena was annoyed.

"The worst was that they insinuated our female corps members were prostitutes. Keeping late nights? Who keeps late hours in terrorized zones? Are we that foolish to play with our lives? Where could we have gotten money to buy hard drugs when we could barely feed with our meagre allowances?"

"Well, I do not believe them. But those vile accusations show how inhuman they are." She hissed loudly.

"The whole nightmare ended when Regina reported the matter to her uncle who is a Brigadier General in the army. He asked her what we had been waiting for. He asked us to complain at the Army base. On getting there, we were turned away, dismissed because we were not dressed in our uniform and asked to come back dressed before we could make any report.

"We ran back and reappeared like ghosts at the base. We recounted all we had been through in the past few days at the school, the local government inspector and zonal inspector's reactions. The Commander was enraged, he was angry we came to him this late and asked a sergeant to go with us under cover. The sergeant dressed in jean and polo and accompanied us to the school.

"He gathered his evidence right from the gate. When we knocked, the gateman opened up and sarcastically referred to us as the stubborn goats saying *"Una don come carry una yeye load commot for here? Abeg make una do so kia kia. I no go dey stress myself come open gate for una o. Na who com be this strong face wey una carry come again? Shebi them don talk say make una no dey bring friend come here, e be like una really carry block for head, dress ojare make I open my gate and carry my market wey I wan shade for customers to come buy jare."*

"Unbelievable! Is it not that old Baba that sells petty items in front of the school's gate? I didn't know that man could be that mean," Efemena said.

"He is the same, Baba Tochi, he could not hide his true behaviour for long. The mean flu got to him as well. The soldier entered, showed his identity card to the school authority, they tried so hard to lie, turning the tables in their favour, but it was too late. The sergeant had seen most of our ordeal and nothing they said could convince him. When we returned to the base, he reported to his superior and I tell you, girl, I didn't know what took over. With the speed of light, the state coordinator and NYSC Headquarters Abuja intervened. The proprietor was summoned to the capital in four hours and he failed to appear.

"As I speak with you, Mena, the state coordinator has ordered us to pack up our belongings and return to the corpers lodge until we are posted to a new place of primary assignment. This NYSC uniform is highly remarkable. The Abuja headquarters warned that if anything happened to us or our wellbeing was threatened, the state would be held responsible." Osaze gulped the last of his drink.

"Wow! I've heard a lot today. How could you have kept these information from me, eh? I'm so impressed with the outcome! Lucky you. Bravo. God bless Regina and her uncle. I am motivated!"

"Look at this girl. Morale!" Osaze said.

"High!" Efemena responded.

"Motivated!" Osaze shouted.

"Motivated! Motivated! Motivated!" They both laughed hysterically.

"Yeah that's the way to go. I need to go," Osaze said, checking his wristwatch.

"Why now? Please stay for lunch."

"Would have loved to but I need to rush, dear. I am on queue at the bank to enroll for my bank verification number."

"Yeah, that reminds me. I'm yet to link mine. The queue at that my bank can be crazily long, the line forms a w-shape."

"Try and do that please, the deadline has been extended. Protect your account from unauthorized access by those cyber frauders and hackers. You don't have to face those unending queues in the banking hall when the policy is good and ready to be implemented. So you see the need for it. Do it quickly, you can't afford your bank account to be inactivate."

Osaze picked up his cap that he hung on an armchair. Jamuike came in at that moment.

"*Corper* Osaze, good to see you in my home, bro. How has NYSC been treating you?"

"My brother, it has been fair enough, welcome back, Sir, I was about to leave."

"Okay, thanks for coming, some other time we will have some good chat here, or at a nice spot."

"Okay brother, bye."

"Yeah, bye for now bro."

"Thank you," Osaze said. Efemena walked him down the stairs. At the gate, he turned around and reprimanded Efemena.

"My friend, what was that? No welcome hug or peck for your husband? Look, Efemena, I don't know what it is but I think you should spice your home. If not for the sake of you both, but for your unborn child who shouldn't come in to this cold atmosphere. Okay?"

"I am sorry, Osaze, thanks for the advice, I got carried away, and I am going through a lot of emotional pain right now."

"Whatever it is, Efemena, free your mind and get a positive grip on it."

"Yeah, I only wish it was that easy, Osaze."

"Hush now. Just be the good girl you've always been. Don't let the demon get your heart. The Lord is your strength, seek refuge in him. We will talk on phone, okay?" They said goodbye and Osaze let himself out.

Back in the house, Jamuike was waiting for her, she looked better than this morning. He could perceive some sweet aroma in the living room, and concluded it was coming from their neighbours. Mrs Bello had prowess in her culinary skills, her restaurant was always filled to the brim with customers and he was sure she was the one filling his tummy with the aroma. He was too tired to go and undress in the bedroom so he sat in the sitting room watching football highlights. The colour of the television was unusually dim. He wondered if the fault was from the setting or the dish's signal. He would rectify the problem before it was time for Efemena to watch her favourite soap opera.

Jamuike was hungry. Efemena waltzed past him towards the kitchen. "How was your session with the doctor today? I hope my babies are doing fine?"

"It was okay. The baby is fine. Thank you. I was not able to finish cooking before Osaze came."

"You don't have to stress yourself, my dear, you need to rest. We could have had tea and toast or something for dinner."

"I'm fine, Jamuike."

"Okay, I can see you are. What are you preparing?"

"Ofe Onugbu."

"My favourite! You just crowned my day, dear. I'll assist you."

"Thank you; I really need help. I have washed the bitter leaf, I put the cocoyam down when I heard the door. It should be cold by now but I will need to heat it up."

"Good, I'll do the pounding afterwards." Efemena led the way into the kitchen.

"Hmmm, I see the stock is ready." Jamuike peeped into the pot. "Dried fish. Are those goat meat? Shaki, pomo, roundabout, liver, stock fish included, and you mashed fresh palm nuts instead of using readymade palm oil? Hulala! Efemena, what got into you today that you went to this extent? It has been long you prepared something elaborate, am I missing something?"

"Well you are not, Oga. I decided to make this soup today. I missed it, and needed a good meal."

"Well, well, well. I feel like I am in paradise, come on let me take it from here, you look like you have had a tedious day. What are we having with it?" he said with excitement and concern.

"Semo, I can't pound yam."

"Alright, Semo is just fine. I can buy yam flour tomorrow or I do the pounding whenever we are going to have it. Please don't use mortar when I am not around. I cannot risk anything happening to you or our baby," he said with all seriousness.

"I also heard that men who help with housework have more

148

libido for sex. I could do most chores and you can repay me in kind?"

"Not in this house, you had better stay away from my kitchen and chores," Jamuike grinned.

Efemena gave him a weak smile and thanked him for his care. After some minutes, the meal was ready. Jamuike pulled a chair to have her sit and dished the food. She thanked him profusely. As they ate, Efemena narrated the story Osaze had told her earlier.

Coincidentally, Jamuike had heard it from one of his colleagues whose wife worked as a teacher at the school. Jamuike was happy that the situation had been resolved. "It would have been a great embarrassment for the community to be tagged oppressive but now the affected corps members would not have an evil report of the state when they returned to their various states."

Jamuike changed the channel to a local station and saw the news that the Oba of Benin had transited into the world of immortals.

"Finally it has been announced," Jamuike referred to the announcement of the king's passage as he flopped into the chair.

Efemena walked into the living room. "Oh Osaze has missed this news. He would not see this because the *corpers* lodge does not have a television."

Jamuike shook his head at the situation and said, "I would forever commend my place of primary assignment as the luxury conferred on us was just too much; we practically begged for the electricity company to take the light so we could stop watching movies and prepare lesson notes. I hope we can improve and make corps members happy here too.

"Let me inform him of this news." Efemena picked her mobile phone from the centre table and dialed Osaze's number. On the third ring, he picked.

"Osaze, it is on the news that your Oba of Benin has died."

"Mena! Sssshhhh. Don't ascribe the 'word' death to the Oba

of Benin. The Home Leopard has only gone home. He has gone to the market or he went for an evening stroll. My king has gone hunting!"

"Ehen?"

"See, let me tell you, Mena, the Oba of Benin never dies but transcends to the world beyond."

"But he died a long time before now, why is it they announced it today?"

"Oba just left the great Benin Kingdom last week into the spirit world according to the oracle."

"Is that so?"

"Madam big tummy, bye."

Efemena laughed into the mouthpiece. Osaze snorted and hung the call.

❦ *Seventeen* ❦

Jamuike was wide awake; he tossed restlessly. He was hungry for that sensational warmth of a woman; that aura, the sweet feel of Efemena's honey pot, his manhood reacted to the sexual pictures he conjured. He just needed to thrust in her right now, to hear that moan of hers, her soft hands scratching his back when he plunged in and out of her tight sheath, touching her womb and giving her fantastic fulfilment.

He thought of going into her room but wondered if Efemena would scratch his eyes out. He put on his boxers, and went to her room. He found her in an irresistible state, looking vulnerable. She wore just panties, her breasts were fuller than the last time he had seen them, the nipples more taut. Her tummy was round. He hovered over her sultry form, caressing her breast slowly with one hand, he used the other to work on her body till she became wet and he almost ran off his wits.

All the while Efemena had been awake, she had been conscious from the moment his feet walked down the corridor. She wondered where he was off to but was alert when he stopped in front of her bedroom door. When he opened, she had felt his naked gaze of desire on her body. She had screamed in her head, "Don't walk out of that door till you make me feel like a woman tonight."

When he began to caress her, she almost ran wild wanting him. She breathed loud. "Take me, take me now and hard."

She had gloried in the feel of the passion emanating from his vigour. Efemena reminded herself she was allowing him because of their baby and not for her pleasure. She needed him to lubricate the passage of her vagina, it had become frigid and cried for grease.

So when Jamuike placed a pillow under her bum, she eased up to make it quicker. With that voluntary movement of consent, he brushed her lips with his, parting them with his tongue, they kissed erotically. While kissing, he thrust into her gently, taking deep strokes. They didn't say anything; just groans, moans, and passionate screams as their orgasm filled the air.

Both sated, Jamuike kissed her and murmured, "Thank you, baby."

"Thank you, too," Efemena breathed the words in his face.

Jamuike lowered his head again to kiss her deeply this time but she warded him off with a knee raised to his chest.

"Jamuike, this should never happen again."

"No, sweetheart, we shouldn't deny ourselves of this beautiful passion we feel for each other," Jamuike pleaded with his eyes.

"No, Jamuike, you lie, I can deny you anything and everything including this baby."

"Now stop that, woman. I will not have you threaten me."

"I mean it, Jamuike. I would rather have a dildo than you in bed."

"That is about the silliest thing I have ever heard in my life. I won't stay here and allow you open your mouth to spew rubbish. Gosh! What a way to freeze our passion. You won't change. I'm out of here."

He came off the bed with the agility of a racer. He stood still for some seconds, then faced Efemena. "Whores do not give emotions so you are not different from your dildo, Mena." Those words made her clench her teeth in fury.

Jamuike left almost the same way he came, muttering inaudible words. Immediately the door closed, Efemena grew furious, empty and cold, but untrue to her words, she and her husband had frequent sensational lovemaking night after night.

Eighteen

Mariam heard a knock on her door and rushed to open it, but was unhappy to see a course mate. She did her best to hide her sadness. "Oh, it's you. Come in." She opened the door wide.

"Were you expecting someone else? I called you before coming, so I'm not an annoying or an unwanted guest. I don't need to step into your room."

She stayed behind the door. "You can just give me the textbook I asked for over the phone so I would leave. Or have you changed your mind?"

"Don't be like that, Susan, I'm sorry, and it's true you are not the one I was expecting, but it does not mean you are not welcome."

"Do not blame me for assuming that; your countenance said it all."

"I'm sorry."

"Apology accepted."

"Okay. Will you stay for a while, I am boiling rice."

"No, thank you, I ate before coming, can you give me the book now?"

"At least take a seat while I get it, I thought you were not vexed with me anymore."

"No, I am not."

"Then come in and take a seat." Susan entered and shut the door. "I'll look for the book." Mariam poured some snacks into a plate and gave to Susan. "Here, please have some."

Susan accepted the kulikuli. "Thank you." She chewed some, and collected the *zobo* drink Mariam offered.

After rummaging through her bookshelves, she brought out the book. "Here, finally found it! Here you go, Susan."

Susan stood up from the bed, and collected it. "Thank you dear, I am greatful."

"You're welcome, dearie, what are friends for."

She smiled. "That's right; I wll make a photocopy and give it back to you after lectures tomorrow. This is just what I need to round up my project."

"How far have you gone with it?"

"Hmmm, still dragging. You know what, Mariam, I will use this term paper for my final project. I will just extend the topic a bit and make the essay more elaborate."

"That is a good idea. If not that I had chosen a much simpler topic, I would have done the same as you. But come to think of it, will your prospective supervisor accept it. What if it is not approved and you are given an entirely different topic?"

"Just wishful thoughts, my dear." She laughed. "No big deal, I was just hoping."

"I would have asked when you became a prophetess or some sort of seer."

"Not at all. Even after all the research, typing, binding and presentation one could be graded a D or E. Ah, some lecturers can be so heartless."

"My sister, it can be heartbreaking, especially when a six-unit course is on the line. Some lecturers are sadists."

"Why should undergraduates have poor grades in their final semester's degree project? Is the supervisor not meant to walk them through every letter in the text to make sure they are correct, accurate and positive within the perimeters of the research? Shouldn't the supervisors be blamed for that shortcoming?"

"I think the supervisor should be sanctioned by their superiors or external bodies for unnecessary failures. A D or E grade should be ascribed to the supervisor's negligence. His or her lack of competency and responsibility will lead naturally to poor performance; because he or she is meant to studiously assess the materials and reports of a supervisee before presentation and final approval of research as stated by the university board of academics. Well, except the student fails at project defence, then it might be, he or she plagiarized or paid someone to write."

"I'll just do my best and leave the rest to God. So, Mariam, tell me, who were you seriously expecting? Is it a guy?"

"Yes, it's a guy,' she said.

"Oh really! Who is he?"

"Tattletale! It is time you take your leave." Susan laughed and told Mariam that one day, she would surely meet the man, and that she did not believe Mariam had a boyfriend.

"Thanks, Mariam, I will take my leave now," Susan smirked.

"You are welcome. I'll see you off." Mariam changed her shorts, and wore a long jean trouser and polo shirt. And they stepped out.

As they approached the bus stop to wait for a commercial vehicle, an ox-blood coloured space bus swerved dangerously close to them that it would have climbed their legs.

Two men pushed an old man out of the moving vehicle and he rolled on the tarred road. He had not reach the ground before he started yelling.

"My bag, my life, all my life savings, and my money! Oh, Chineke!"

"Get a hold of yourself, Sir, you are bleeding, don't hurt yourself further," Susan cautioned him.

"Please, Sir, stop, what happened?" Susan and Mariam held his hands and tried to drag him off the road as motorists honked for him to leave the road.

"Susan, help me hold my phone." She handed it over to Susan.

"Put it inside your handbag and let us carry him up." Other people came to join them as they lifted him up.

"What happened, Sir?"

"Oh, my money! My life, my savings, they are all in there." He placed his hands on his head.

"Your savings, you mean they made away with your money?" Mariam asked.

"Yes, my money o, I need my bag back. What will I tell my wife, my children? How do I face a new beginning? These people have ruined me. One chance has caught me. My bag is inside that vehicle. My gratuity I want to use in starting up a business. God, help me stop them. I'll die here. Oh, somebody will carry my corpse."

"Sorry, sorry," sympathizers consoled him.

They were still trying to calm him when a policeman drove the bus back. He scrambled to his feet not minding his bruised elbow. A young man stopped his bicycle alongside.

"My bag, my bag." He rushed in.

"Officer, thank you. Oh! This is my life." He weighed it, and firmly wrapped his arms round it.

"You should thank this gentleman here." He beckoned the biker. "He saw when these criminals," he pointed at the handcuffed driver and two other men in the bus, "shoved you out. He rode fast, reached our checkpoint, and reported. We blocked the road immediately and caught them easily."

"Oh, nna, dalu. This is amazing," the man said to his saviour. "Your heart heard my humble cry."

Mariam and Susan looked at the young man with admiration and gratefulness.

"That was brilliant of you," Susan said.

"Yes, you have done well," Mariam added.

"Nno, my son, God bless you forever. You shall have no cause to encounter ill lucks on your journey."

"Amen, Sir, I'm glad I saved the situation."

"Congratulations, young man, such agility and assistance is what forces need. Your likes should be bred in the institution," the policeman said patting him on his shoulder.

156

"Ah, Sir, I don't want to be a force man. I've a comfortable civilian life."

"Mariam, that bus is going to Ariaria. I should get going." Susan waved at the conductor whose head peeked out to bellow his routes.

"Alright, safe okay; I will come soon and check out weaves in your shop."

"Okay, I'm expecting you very soon." Susan entered the bus and Mariam waved her off.

With each passing day it became a long, long way from home for Efemena. Every of her fellow corps member would return to their homes at their own free will. Some may find good starts here, be it in wedlock or employment. She used to pray for a hearty homecoming, but now she had to find solace here. Maybe her business would flourish, when she resigned to fate. The town was very industrious, traders from North, South, and West always export goods from there, and probably she would get a suite at the complex. God willing, she would prosper.

Final clearance would commence in less than eighteen days. She sat idly in her department and stared at the television. A text message from the CLO brought her back to consciousness. All corps members were to assemble at the zonal office for a meeting by four o'clock and attendance was mandatory. Efemena got up and left for the zonal office. INEC was employing the services of corps members. They were to handle the collection of the temporary voter's card, issuance of the permanent voter's card and would be trained for a week on how to register and produce temporary voters' cards.

Efemena looked forward to the national duty, another amazing experience in her service year. After a long wait for their supervisory distribution officer, they came together to decide on how to move because their INEC supervisor did not make provisions for that. With murmurings, they strolled to hire a bus. They got to the head polling centre where working materials were distributed. They were given ink, election voters register, pen and water gum.

The supervisory distribution officer instructed them to come back to submit daily reports on how many permanent voters cards and temporary voters cards were issued, by four o'clock in the evening. In case they did not report at the stipulated time, they were to go to the government secretariat for compulsory submission no later than six o'clock.

Efemena had been informed that her polling unit had more voters. The community had a governorship aspirant and she needed not worry because she would be treated with great hospitality. She gathered her materials to move to Omuobiakwa when two gentlemen came around and introduced themselves as indigenes of Omuobiakwa; the town she was posted. They had come to pick her. She entered the car with the other corps members that had been posted there.

The town hall was arranged neatly with pews. The citizens were well coordinated; they searched for their names on the voters register, tendered their temporary voter's card *or* two passports and filled attestation forms. The people were politically inclined; elders and youths came out *en masse* to collect their permanent voters' cards and they waited patiently to collect the permanent card. Efemena was happy to see aged men and women with their temporary voters' cards intact while most youths had tattered cards or had misplaced them. Soon, Efemena knew why the elders guarded their cards jealously. After collecting their permanent voters' cards, they asked the Councillor, who was present at that time, for food money and transport fare. It was a funny sight, as he had to empty his pockets. The first day had a good turnout and Efemena looked forward to another day.

The second day, she picked up her materials with no money from INEC. She was at the town hall before 11 am with more cards to disburse, the day seemed hectic from the onset. People she left unattended to the previous evening, plus new arrivals, kept her busy. The atmosphere was indeed different. Many people clustered around the table, obstructing air from the window. Efemena did not know from whose face sweat dripped on her arm and within seconds, it itched like yam peels. She stopped shuffling cards to clean it off and scratch the spot. When she could not bear it, Efemena told them to move away from the table, get seated, or stand some feet away from her table. She bought meat pie, drinks, and fruits to combat her hunger as she dealt with the impatient crowd.

Her mood became tense when some overbearing youths came to collect some permanent voters' cards forcefully. When she refused, a hooligan stood up from a seat at the far end of the hall to tell her that was not the way things worked there. She was just an agent; they were in charge in the community and not the other way round. His bullying failed to goad Efemena into obeying. The overbearing youths would have constituted a menace if not for the intervention of the councillor. He chastised their ungentle attitude towards a lady.

The councillor apologized and made them do likewise. Efemena felt a bit threatened; it dawned on her that she had not seen any security agent that was supposed to be assigned to her polling unit from the Nigerian Police Force or Nigerian Security and Civil Defense Corps or any other security agency mandated to enforce and maintain law and order throughout the exercise.

She felt unsecured. Efemena put up an act of bravery telling them she was not afraid of them and that they dared not push her limits. Efemena was afraid; despite the Police station being a few blocks away, no officer came around to ensure her wellbeing. Maybe they felt that their nearness would deter the people from causing troubles; she hoped that was the reason for their absence.

Efemena became at ease when the boys came again to apologize, and promised that there would not be a repeat. Efemena was impressed with a man who came without his temporary voter's card. She refused him his permanent voter's card until he did the needful. The gentleman exited the hall with a bright smile. Later, she was told he was the governorship aspirant.

On the last day, Efemena had attended first mass so that she could be in time at her unit. The great number of the remaining permanent voters' cards made her early. The queue was longer than other days. It was obvious a lot of pressure was on the supervisor. She called Efemena to inform her that everyone else was meeting at the local government secretariat for final reports and total submission of materials. It was not until six o'clock that Efemena rounded up as more people trooped in from the moon, stars and clouds.

She pleaded that she needed to leave. They could see she was married and an expectant mother. They apologized and gave her money for diapers and provisions with fruits. Efemena thanked them and prayed that the community would produce the next governor in the coming elections. They were cooperative.

After all was concluded at the local government secretariat, they were paid nine thousand naira (₦9000) as against the fifteen thousand naira (₦15000) they were promised. Efemena lamented: "There is corruption everywhere, cheats in different forms and at various levels; thieves in disguise, greedy wolves in sheep's contented faces."

❦‖ *Nineteen* ‖❦

Barely a week to her POP, Efemena made good sales. The biggest market complex had August buyers as corps members invaded shops and makeshift stalls. It was the largest market in West Africa nicknamed *'the China of Africa'* because of its large varieties of footwears, furniture, clothing and textiles. They produced great designer clothes and shoes, exquisite furniture which a house or hotel could be decorated with in classic and affordable tastes. Ariaria International Market was a structured open-air market located in the heart of Aba. It boasts over two million traders with specialization in all kinds of goods, services and artistic works making use of local and imported raw materials.

Corps members were scattered all over the market, picking designer wears to go for job interviews. Some bought bedsheets and pillow cases with duvet, curtains, throw pillows, and foot mats made from fluffy materials. On a daily basis, big trucks were loaded with these manufactured items to other cities within Nigeria and were also exported. Ariaria was the famous market where intending brides came for their shopping. Event decorators bought chair covers and other materials for beautification. Schools contracted fashion designers to sew coats for its students, manufacture customized shoes and stockings amongst many everyday individual wears.

Corps members were enthusiastic, hoping the labour market had good deals for them. Some envisioned getting employment immediately; some had job appointments, while others were uncertain of their employability status.

Prior to this month, thousands of unemployed graduates and serving corps members had applied in the Immigration recruitment drive and many lives were lost during the examination exercise. Jobs in Nigeria were diamond and gold. Even a cleaning job was a hot shot. Efemena had been advised by Mrs Comfort to be cautious in her search for good jobs. She had given Efemena a diary of her life after service; she had not been prudent with her savings. She gallantly applied for jobs in the four regions of the nation, travelling here and there for interviews.

This made her exhaust the money she saved from her NYSC monthly allowance on transportation, buying provision in houses of friends she put up with. Within a month, she became a beggar. None of the interviews successfully led to her becoming even a contract staff.

She became a full time nanny, taking care of her parents and younger siblings. Sometimes, her younger ones disregarded her. They frowned at her presence; they saw her as a food snatcher, shortening their food ration. It would have been sufficient if she had gone away. She was supposed to have enthroned the mantle of capability and not become a liability.

Efemena gained a lot from Mrs Comfort. She was not the only one lamenting about the strenuous challenges after service. The various skills acquired during service were not sufficient. They had trained youths in the arts of bead making, soap making and baking, but there was no capital and necessary assets, to start up an enterprise.

Perhaps, the allowance paid monthly for upkeep was what ex-corps members were meant to pump into business ventures. A business idea without capital is like vision without action. Only a surviving warrior can coherently tell the experience of a war. Most corps members believed that after surviving the Nigerian university and escaping three weeks drilling on camp, they could survive anything. Efemena shrugged, POP was around the corner and not even the darkest cloud could disrupt her bright future.

✳   ✳   ✳   ✳   ✳

POP was here, and Efemena could not suppress her joy. She was lying on her bed. It was just like yesterday even though it seemed so far at some point, as though everything was stuck on one time. It had arrived; the day she would obtain her discharge certificate. She realized her Batch would have 'COC' collection of certificate and not POP.

The way they missed out on endurance trek and emergency fire outbreak and false alarm, they would miss the fun of passing out parade. The endurance walk would have taken place outside camp, with security and health officials in tow, to escort and be on guard to avert dangers or help anyone. But it was cancelled because of the frequent threats in the 'poverty trapped north' and now, no passing out parade at the usual state capital nationwide, it was going to be 'collection of certificate'. All corps members would assemble at their zonal headquarters to collect their discharge certificates. Some traditional cultures were eluded during Efemena's service year. Efemena had looked forward to seeing her friends she last saw on camp and now, she may never see them again. Boko Haram was threatening the nation's safety, releasing fire and brimstone in the North. For security purposes, Federal government had mandated a low key passing out ceremony to avoid incidences that would cost lives. She pranced around with her slightly bulging tummy, missing friends she had known for a year.

Efemena wished the NYSC scheme did not happen. She wished life never came in phases and one must meet awesome and annoying persons that may never be seen again. She moved around greeting and hugging her friends. Boxes and bags had been stalled at motor parks, some corps members set to travel to various destinations. Some could not stay one more night, out of pain of having to say goodbye or to quickly possess their awaiting offices, or celebrate with family and friends at home. Efemena would remain when almost everyone else had gone. She was stuck where she was, forming another life. It was all going to be good, she consoled herself as tears filled her eyes.

❧ Twenty ❧

Some relationships are like a game of chess. Commitment amongst opposite sexes can sometimes be as flippant as a popular consumer commodity. The relationship status of some people often changes at will, like a chameleon, to adapt to and be accepted in any particular environment or situation.

The words 'I want sex' were now said to mean love. Affections had no humble intention. The pronouncement of love from one person to the other could be true on the surface with so much evidence comprising physical and emotional (sexual and gift enticements verbal and oral endowments), but devoid of authentic feelings.

Sometimes, the powerful effect of loving someone can knock out every molecule of common sense in the one in love. The mind, heart, thinks and beats only for that moment of affection.

"Do you have to leave? You can actually sleep over." The man in his late twenties did not say a word to Mariam.

"Babe." She tapped his left wrist and joined him to tie his sneaker's laces. "I have my freedom now, you can stay the night," she urged him.

"That's dangerous, Mariam."

"But what's the danger here, Elvis?"

He shook his head, "I have said it countless times, babe. Do you know we could get naughty and ...?"

"And so what if we end up making love? Are we not in a relationship? Sooner or later we are bound to anyway."

"The sooner would only be when I make you my wife."

"Oh, come on!" Mariam was fuming. "First you asked me to get an HIV/AIDS test and you have been with the results for the past three months, yet you don't touch me."

"Mariam."

"What is wrong, am I not attractive enough? I know I'm not ugly." She rubbed her breast on his chest. Elvis groaned at his arousal and stiffened his arms not to smooch her.

His voice was hoarse when he spoke. "Mariam, stop, just stop please; I try to cool but it's killing me right now. You will push me to take you on this floor."

"Take me, baby." She pulled of her silky gown from her shoulder and like a warrior stood in the pool of her garment.

Elvis feasted his eyes on her body for some minutes. Mariam watched his member rise at her sensual command. She sneaked a hand in his shirt, and caressed his nipples. She smiled wantonly when she felt his pulse booming like an exclusive club speaker.

"Stop, Mariam." He roughly snatched her hands away. "You're courting danger for yourself."

"Oh! Is it that I'm cursed or just graciously repulsive?" She glanced at her well rounded hips and her luscious full breast and begged to be loved.

"Oh, you are just damn too religious!"

"Thank you," he gritted his teeth in annoyance. "I beg to take my leave now, I have to be at the club with my friends."

"Oh, you can go to hell for all I care. It would sound reasonable you're attending fellowship that's why you deny me sex."

She bent down and wore her clothes. Elvis had a surge between his thighs as he watched her buttocks.

"I'll see you next weekend." Mariam said nothing. "I better go now." She flung her face towards the wall and hissed.

Obviously she wouldn't see him to the door, so Elvis let himself out. He winced in pain and undid his zippers inside the car. He felt cool as the air conditioner circulated and he drove off; thinking he would have to meet Mariam's parents by second semester.

"I'll be doomed if I don't act fast," Mariam pondered as she thought of ways to get rid of the fetus in her womb.

It'll be hard to convince him the pregnancy is his now that her plan to get him in bed did not click. She flung herself on the bed and stared hard at a grey gecko poised to catch a cockroach. She was running out of time. He could propose in the next twenty years if he pleases, Mariam thought and smiled. She finalized aborting the issue, she could have more sweet time with her father and they won't be in disagreement anymore.

A few months after POP, Efemena delivered a cute boy, a replica of his father. He had his father's paternal birthmark on the same spot; the right side of his breast, a little below the nipple. People came in droves to congratulate the parents. Efemena was glad the guests were wise enough not to carry her baby from his cradle. She did not have to worry about her baby being handled with unwashed hands as it would be awkward if you asked them to wash.

Her mother had warned her not to accept money from anyone that had a big navel; that they would pass the hugeness to her baby.

Efemena's stomach was flat as if she was never pregnant. Mrs Aruegodore had told Jamuike to have the nurses give her *Ogogoro* to drink, which instantly flushed any waste from her tummy. Jamuike personally threw the placenta into a sewer when it was handed over to him by a nurse. Nobody was there except Mrs Comfort to take care of her and the baby until her father grudgingly gave in and allowed her mother. Her mother had cried day in day out, pleading she should at least go to see them. She was saddened and could not bear thoughts of not nursing her daughter and grandson. Aruegodore swallowed his pride. He allowed his wife go along with many provisions, clothing and also a message to Efemena telling her he knew it was not her intention to get married, especially with the unplanned pregnancy. If she was not happy, she could come home whenever she wanted. He was willing to send her to any school of her choice for postgraduate study. She was his bone and flesh.

✻ ✻ ✻ ✻ ✻

Mrs Comfort had been doing great until the arrival of Efemena's mother. The touch of a mother was however different. Her recipe for pepper soup had no rival, the medicinal condiments were unrivaled as she knew the right spices to brew.

It was time to bathe the baby, and Mrs Aruegodore came calling "Mena, put water on fire. I hope you have stove in your home because I need it smoking hot."

"Haba, what would you need such for? I do not see any chicken in sight. Whose feathers do you want to pluck eh?"

"Efemena, I have no plans of plucking anything; you and my grandson need special bath. I am going to massage your bodies. When I am done, *you go know say hand touch you.*" She smiled.

"But Mrs Comfort has been doing all that. What is your point, Izu? Are you saying she has not been doing a good job in taking care of us?"

"Never mind my child, I'm just saying there are some things left undone that I your mother have to accomplish. Mena, listen to the woman that gave birth to you. I know better, I only want to perform my duty as a mother and grandmother. I am grateful to Mrs Comfort."

"Okay. Do your thing." Efemena went into the kitchen and brought out the kettle.

"This is not it, Mena, this size of kettle cannot produce the

168

amount of water we need."

"Is it not to bathe me and the baby?"

"Not just bathing, but massage as well. I hope you have been sitting on hot water, you need to heal that birth house."

"I normally use hot water to bathe," Efemena replied.

"So you have not been sitting on hot water? If you do not take care of your vagina, it will affect you when you meet with your husband. You might fart during sex."

"Haba, Izu!"

"Mena, a baby came out of your private part. It needs to be closed and firm again for your husband to enjoy intimacy with you and you as well. You don't want your husband feeling he's dipping into a borehole, do you?"

"I wash with warm water," she insisted.

"You will sit on it today, and every other day till it is tight and firm." Efemena made a disgruntled sigh. She would have to unpack the bucket she had used two days after her baby's delivery. The heat worked well but was unbearable to the flesh.

"But, Izu, I am still bleeding. It thumps nearly to a pool."

"Are you serious?" Enatomare was surprised.

"Yes, I am wearing pad at the moment. That is why I stopped heating it; it makes a mess."

"That's strange. Did you recently mate with your husband?"

"No, I am still sore. It is unheard of to have sex so soon. I love my life."

"Very strange, you are not supposed to have your flow until your husband meets you again on bed; it has been so in our lineage."

"That's odd."

"If you meet him after a while, it is then you start menstruating. I will make you sit on it and massage your body after the baby's bath," she said holding a small pot in hand.

"Are these all the pots you have in your house?"

"Yeah." Efemena turned away from her mother to return the kettle.

"Hmm. It is my fault, and this is also because you were not properly married."

"I don't like this please; I don't like the sound of that. I'm legally married to my husband." She showed her ring finger to her mother. "I am Mrs Efemena Jamuike Akuabia."

"Don't be too fast, young lady. A child must first crawl before he begins to walk. Growth comes in stages, and so does marriage. Who did your husband pay your bride price to? Was he ever formally introduced to your family? Who issued the marriage list to him, who did your husband present a box of clothes to? Did we prepare Owofugbo soup for your husband's family?"

"Oh, Izu! What has pot got to do with these traditional values, please just stop, you are going too far," she was annoyed.

"I will hang on your word 'values'. Such marriage rites are highly valued in our culture. If both of you had obeyed customs and traditions, your home would have been filled with different sizes of pots; you would have received presents from the guests."

She murmured. "Is it people's pot that would make my marriage work eh? I will borrow a pot as big as this house from my neighbour, she has lots of them stored in the garage downstairs."

"Borrow, a married woman borrowing pot?" She pointed at the small and medium sized pots "Are those the pots you prepare food with when your husband's friends or relatives visit?"

"It's not up to a year we got married. We are yet to entertain that large number of guests. I cook meals that serve me and my husband, and perhaps one more person."

"Hmm. Mena! Mena!"

"Izu, it is okay, let's manage the borrowed pot for today. I promise we will get bigger pots tomorrow."

"Do that. I would be pleased if you have them in your kitchen before I leave."

"Definitely, I will."

Efemena brought in the pot and poured water in it. She asked her mother why she decided to light the stove when she could easily use the gas.

"Mena, when a blender is used to grind pepper, it loses some of its nutrients because one must add water to it, unlike that grinding stone. So it's with stove and gas; if there was firewood or coal pot available, I would opt for either because it guarantees steamed water."

"Hmmm, I think I get what you mean. The difference is clear. I always think the reason why the jollof rice at parties taste delicious is because it is prepared with firewood. There is this aroma and taste it gives to it." She smiled. "Was that why you had an outdoor kitchen built at home, Izu?"

"That's right, Mena, I am not confident in the taste of my meals when I don't prepare them with charcoal or firewood, especially soup! Even your father can tell the difference whenever I cook late and have to use gas. Bring the water to your bedroom when it is ready, dear. I'm going to speak with your father for a while." They both left the kitchen.

Enatomare met Jamuike on her way. "Oghome. How are you, my son?"

"I am fine, Izu. How are you today, Ma?"

"Very well, my dear. Thanks for the gifts you sent to my room."

"Ah, it is nothing, Ma, I cannot appreciate you enough."

"Okay, my in-law. You have done well. God shall continue to bless your union, and give you more children."

"Amen, Izu, Amen."

"Alright, I am off to my room.

"Okay, Ma."

Enatomare closed the windows of Efemena's bedroom in order to make the room's temperature warm. The baby's umbilical cord had fallen off; Mrs Comfort had expertly treated it by rubbing alcohol, the spot healed finely.

She laid the baby astride her thighs; lying on his tummy. She took hot water from a bucket and poured into another which was cold. Enatomare mixed the water by checking its warmth

171

with her wrist and elbow. She used a soft sponge to wash the baby. She dabbed a little ointment on the baby's circumcision wound.

Efemena wore a long face. "My baby has not excreted for more than four days now," Efemena said.

"No need to be worried, he is trying to be fat. If he excretes every day; he is likely not to gain weight. Some babies can stay without excreting for a week in order to grow big."

"I am worried. I think it's almost a week now."

"Okay, in that case, get me lux soap. I hope you have at home."

"Yes, I have it." She retrieved a bar of lux soap in the baby's drawer near her wardrobe.

"Here." She handed the soap to her mother. Enatomare broke some particles off and inserted then in the baby's anus. After a while, Ifeanyi began to excrete easily. He smiled and giggled at his grandma; babbling.

Efemena was fascinated and asked her mother how that worked. Enatomare told her it was a method that has worked for mothers and midwives for a long time.

"Mena, you can now go and heat up the native pot, and get me seven *Udah Uwentia*–negro pepper. Make sure you mash it gently in the mortar so that only the shafts are pieced, do not break the seeds."

Efemena did as she was told. She brought the pieces which she wrapped in a handkerchief and tied firmly. Efemena carried the tub with water and flung it in from the bathroom's entrance. Her mother warned her not to do that again. She was to carefully put the tub on the floor, and let the water pour out.

"What is wrong with the way I poured the water?"

"It is bad for the baby. It might deform his body. It is like throwing him with the bath water."

"Hmm. There is nothing someone will not hear as a mother. Oghene!"

Efemena placed a pot on the stove. She dabbed the tied

handkerchief inside a container filled with coconut oil.

"Now press the handkerchief to the pot." Efemena complied. "Press it harder."

"Okay." The room was filled with pepper soup aroma. Efemena handed it to her mother, who repeatedly touched it to her cheeks to test its hotness. She felt it was okay, and pressed it to the baby's navel.

"Careful oh. Won't that hurt him?" Efemena winced for her baby.

"It won't, Mena, can't you see he's happy?" The baby was smiling. "His navel will heal faster with this and Nospamin. It must not be only after bath you massage his navel with it. You can apply it anytime you notice he feels stomach discomfort. And use this particular handkerchief until he is healed." She repeated the massage three more times, and she was done. She dressed the baby and handed him over to his mother.

The way Enatomare massaged her daughter's body had Efemena wondering if she was her biological mother, because she mercilessly slapped smoking water on every part of her. Her mother made sure she sat for thirty minutes over hot water for her private part to heal.

"Degwo," she said gratefully as her baby was still smiling.

"Vrendo, Omoteme." Enatomare stood up from the small stool, pecked Ifeanyi on both cheeks. She adjusted his cap to cover every strand of his hair. "I'm off to bed now. Those drugs I took are having an effect on me."

"Okay, do have a splendid rest."

Efemena heard a knock on her door as she was putting the baby to sleep. "Izu, did you forget something?" she asked.

"It is me. Mena."

"Oh Jamuike, it is you."

"Can I come in for some minutes? There is something important I would like to discuss with you."

"Sure, come in."

Jamuike opened the door noiselessly. Pecked their son lightly and went to her window from where he gazed at the darkness outside.

He spoke without looking at her. "Mena, I was not eavesdropping but I heard your mother talk about how improper our marriage is."

"Do not bother, Ike, is that why you came here?"

"It troubles me a lot, Mena. Though your mother had said those words with a good heart, they are pains of an unfulfilled mother, I understand. I know as well that I have not done right by not marrying you the proper way." Efemena looked downcast as Jamuike approached her slowly.

He placed his hands gently on her shoulders, and guided her gently so she sat on the bed, he did likewise. "Please, Mena, tell me about your customs with regards to marriage rites."

"But what's the point, Jamuike?"

"Sssh. I still need to know." Efemena took a deep breath, and started talking.

"Before marriage, the ritual known as *Udi Arhovwaje* takes place in the ancestral home of the bride or a patrilineal relation, as agreed. We could have been married in either my paternal grandparent's house or my father's house."

"Okay?" She didn't say anything after two minutes. "Go on, Mena, I'm listening."

"On an agreed date, the man goes with his relatives and friends to the bride's place for formal introduction. You were supposed to come to my father's home bringing gifts of drinks, salt, kola nut and we would cook to entertain guests. Afterwards, your people would come with the list presented for the marriage formalities."

"I see. That is similar to mine."

"Formal approval for marriage is given by the bride's parents or whoever is representing. They would pray with the gin you have brought that my father's ancestors should bless us with health, children and wealth. It is only after this marriage rite that the husband can claim a refund of bride price if the marriage

174

fails. As at now, you owe my family nothing. I am just a free item in your house."

Jamuike winced at the hurt in her voice. "If you had settled my price, it is believed that the ancestors were a witness to our marriage. It is only the physical body that is sent to her husband in the marriage, her *Erhi* remains in the family home. And do you know that, in our culture, a woman is brought back to be buried in her family home when she dies?"

"Really?"

Efemena nodded her head slowly. "Except my son requests my body to be laid at rest in his father's hometown. And it must be under his roof, the very house he built that I would be buried in or a house he built for me."

"Wow. It sounds funny but not weird though," he added as Efemena batted her eyelids at him. "Our son shall be wealthy so that he can keep my wife here forever."

Sensing he had offended her, he tried to veer the course of their discussion. "So when I finally come to pay your bride price, I get to eat *Ukhodo*, yam and unripe plantain prepared with goat meat; and spiced thickly with lemon grass."

"You are definitely going to eat Owofugbo soup as marriage rites."

"Yes! Oil soup with starch. You know, baby, I love that Owo soup. No qualms if I don't get Ukhodo; I will just eat the Owo soup with yam and plantain. The tasteful prospect of eating this meal makes me want to get married traditionally today, sweetheart. However, Banga soup is still my favourite anytime."

Efemena stood up abruptly. "Jamuike, I think you should go now. I and our baby need to rest and it has been a long day. "Good night, Ike."

"Right. I'm out. Good night Mena." Jamuike kissed their son, and bowed his head to Efemena as he unhappily left the room.

Enatomare was with them for three months. Her husband called frequently to ask about Efemena and her baby. Efemena maintained her bedroom despite her mother's disapproval of the arrangements since she arrived. Enatomare had a cordial and motherly interaction with Jamuike, she saw him as her son; he was just a month younger than her first son. She saw Jamike as an awesome man and prayed they found undying love and care for each other as true husband and wife.

She was worried about her daughter's disposition to her husband. "What happened between you and Jamuike is already done, but you can make it work. You can both find love and understanding." After a while, she left the East. She took a lot of pictures to the family at home.

Twenty-one

Being an ex-corps member meant no more work at the local government. Efemena became a partial housewife and mother. Her routine were going to the hospital for post-natal, her baby's welfare and her business.

Three months later, all her efforts to get a well-paying job proved abortive. Being a nursing mother did not help as most employers sought to employ singles. Jamuike's moves to get her retained at the local government as a regular staff were futile. He did not even have the influence to get his wife the position of a messenger.

NYSC's umbrella no longer shielded Efemena from the frenzy rains and scathing sun of business. The awareness that she was no longer a corps member made most of her customers pay her late, unlike the past when they paid her fairly on time because they feared she might call soldiers on them if they failed or delayed unnecessarily. Efemena began experiencing poor business conditions in the environment. Sales were slow; her customers demanded for supply and refused to pay thereby tying down her capital and making her spend her profit.

Jamuike took to transport business with his car after office hours; he became a commercial driver. Efemena would settle for nothing less than the best. She never planned on having a child she would not be able to feed, and now with her slow business, she tasked Jamuike like a first class nagging wife. He had made her to remain in this town, so he must drink from her misfortune. She made his life uneasy.

Jamuike plied the highways, major roads and streets. At times, he went as far as the neighbouring states. His wife had quit using her money to purchase any household item. He never blamed her; he worked tirelessly hoping to make his wife and son comfortable. If he did not provide money for meals, remnants awaited him in the kitchen. If lucky, he ate the bread and fruits he bought on his way home. He cursed the day he met and sowed his seeds in Efemena's womb, but he blessed her for always looking out for their son.

She had become a tigress overnight, they quarreled about everything. All his earnings from the transport business went into Efemena's purse to purchase foodstuffs, diapers, clothes, milk, medications, and cosmetics. No change to buy himself some bottles on Friday nights any more. He could no longer afford to hang out with his friends on Friday nights; his life was messed up. The local government owed its workers salaries of three months.

Ifeanyi Junior Akuabia became a year old. The birthday party was a colouration of the neighbourhood. There were big cakes, small chops, grottos, and clowns, with adults and children in attendance. Jamuike disclosed his worries over expenses before the date, but Efemena would have none of it.

"Efemena, this extravagance of yours can be postponed to another year, why don't you understand me? The state governors last week said they plan to reduce minimum wage due to the dwindling economy. There is a reduction in federal allocation."

"Pets at government house are catered for with more than twenty thousand naira a day; so why won't our son have a fabulous bash, Ike? Enough please."

This was her idea of an ideal celebration for her child's one year birthday, to be an awesome, unforgettable moment. If she did not have the finances she would borrow. She would have aborted the baby if she thought for once he was going to grow up in penury. She admonished Jamuike to hush his fears of how they feed after the party.

Jamuike became a perpetual driver. He virtually wore different shirts and one trouser for a week. He was working round the clock; his old acquaintances could mistake him for a far older man. The only betrayal to his recent appearance was that he lacked grey hairs.

Efemena started her business again in full swing. She went to distant towns and other states to deliver goods to her numerous new and old clients. Her business was flourishing and she was happy once again. Often she made a detour to pay her family a short visit amidst her business trips with Ifeanyi.

Jamuike became a full-time baby-sitter whenever she was away and did not take Ifeanyi with her. He dropped the kid in school and picked him up afterwards. This new routine could not allow him drive to distant places anymore; he only worked within the town and made lesser money.

He became a nanny, professional cook and dad. A few times, when he passed through Ifeanyi's school at closing hour, he pleaded with passengers to pick up his son quickly, at such times he had reserved the passenger's seat for him. Ifeanyi grew every day into a smaller version of his father.

Efemena never failed to buy Ifeanyi all the things money could get. She was the best material mother one could ever ask for with so much love. She nurtured her son with every love she could shower every time she was at home. Ifeanyi had toys: race cars, bike, games, guns, horse, and several kid stuff. He was a bevy of envy to children in the neighbourhood. He attended one of the best schools; his lunch basket was never empty. Efemena kept the refrigerator filled with groceries. Once in a while, they went out as a happy family to amusement parks and eateries.

On the third week of her arrival from a business trip, she

informed Jamuike she was traveling out of the country in the next two weeks. Jamuike let loose his pent-up anger at her. He lashed out insults, called her a business prostitute. In retaliation Efemena called him a fool and for the first time, she received a punch. The punch made her dumb for some minutes. She burst into tears and screamed attracting the attention of their neighbours.

Mr and Mrs Bello helped themselves into the house; they were baffled at Jamuike's unusual behaviour. Mr Bello reminded Jamuike how barbaric it was to hit a woman, while his wife sat Efemena down, and wiped her tears.

Efemena's left eye was swollen. Her face marked with Jamuike's fist. It was 3:37 pm and someone would have to go and pick Ifeanyi from school. Jamuike was still in rage and Efemena was in a bad shape. Mr Bello whose children attended the same school offered to pick up their son. He secured the permit card from Jamuike. Mrs Bello stayed to treat Efemena's face, she applied some ice blocks she found in their deep freezer, rubbed balm to ease the pains and gave her some pain killers.

❧‖ *Twenty-two* ‖❧

After Mr Bello handed over Ifeanyi and his children to his wife, he took Jamuike for a drive. They drove through the town and finally stopped at its outskirt and entered a local bar. On his second bottle, Jamuike broke into tears. He allowed the tears roll freely down his cheeks and his lips absorbed them with no shame. Mr Bello refilled his glass without saying a word until Jamuike broke the long silence.

"Bello, I feel so wretched right now. I see Karma dealing mercilessly with me. I have dated different women in the past and none has ever showed me a nickel of hell as Efemena is doing. At a point in my life, I felt I was too handsome to belong to one woman. I prided myself as the lady charmer and then, I got enthralled by Efemena's beauty. I was smitten by her jovial nature, brilliance and sexiness. I yearned to get intimate with her. I got my wish and more, my lovely son. Of all the ladies I dated, no one ever conceived for me, none to my knowledge so you would understand why I wanted to marry Efemena and keep the baby because I did not want to risk my chances. I felt lucky. I forced my wife to keep the pregnancy against her wish. I could not allow our son be born out of wedlock because the hatred Efemena had for me then, she would have forever denied me of my son. I had my way with her by threats. I was too self-centred. I did not care to go with her wishes and did not even go to her parents for blessings for our union. I never did right by not paying her bride price the traditional way. As I speak

181

with you, I am yet to know the birthplace and village of my wife. I have only had the opportunity of speaking with my father in-law on phone which was a less friendly conversation, and the last communication was the text message I sent, thanking him for granting my mother in-law permission to come be with my family. I know you might be wondering where I am leading with my stories, I will tell you more. I had a great lady who could have been my missing rib, my heartbeat and soul mate. She was right in front of me but I walked past her; she was hanging to my arm but I let her slip. She was spread beautifully on my palm and I blew her off like withered roses. Her name is Janet and I called her Angel. She was the light in my world; I loved and still love her so much. I ran a shop when I was younger; her tailoring shop was beside mine. From neighbours we became friends and then lovers. I could go to the market and entrust my goods under her wing to sell, she was very industrious and a good saleswoman. When I gained admission into the university, which I sponsored myself, I wondered how I would run my shop which was my only means of livelihood and go to school. I could not afford to employ a sales girl or boy, and even if I did, the loyal ones are dinosaurs. My angel offered to help me out. Like a bird built a safe nest for its eggs, Janet turned my venture around for good. My business flourished, and to a point we both decided to demolish the wall demarcating our shops. Subsequently, she let go of some of her apprentices and stationed some of her machines in my shop to sew for some exclusive customers. She ran the business to a profitable stage, added more stocks and the shop boasted all kinds of consumer goods. I graduated, went for my national youth service. My late uncle, Eze Chimobi, God rest his soul, helped me secure my job as a court clerk. Postgraduate study followed immediately after, and I completed a master's degree in Public and International Relations. I went from the parlour and room to a two-bedroom flat meant for bachelors only. I wanted to live the life I had not been opportuned in the past, my life had revolved around business, academics with little or no fun. I yearned to feel how living life to the fullest could be, spending money on blazers, Italian suits and shoes, with women flocking around. I bought a *tokunbo* car and my status upgraded. I intentionally took that apartment because it would restrict Janet from staying over at will; I wanted to put her at arm's length to have more freedom. I retained my old house where she resided, and I spent few weekends with her. A day came, and my angel drummed some motherly advice in my ears. She told me she had suspected that I would put up such attitude in the long run. I am a man and may need to test other fishes in the river. She condemned my reckless expenditure which could run down the establishment. She warned me to reduce my excessive spending, or else the business will be ruined. I should have thought of laying a foundation on my land to build our own home, we could have managed the room and parlour instead of renting a flat and buying a car. I told her bluntly I was not prepared to get married until the next three years or more when I would be ready to give my wife and children the best. I knew I was hurting her but I wanted freedom. She said little in response, telling me I could do as I wished if it is what I truly wanted, who was she to object, that my intentions are best known to me. She respected my decision and from that day forth, we never talked about marriage. I began to notice her spirited love for me was souring, I did not want to talk about it with her or I might just be giving in to a speedy holy matrimony. My business died as she fell out of love with me. I squandered both capital and profit, a petty trader was better than me. Once more, she barricaded her shop. But this time around she rented it out, while I sold mine later. We stayed apart for some months, no calls, no visits, and no physical contact. I began to miss the light of my world; the vacuum in my heart became open. I ached for care and needed comfort from her bosom. I got to our apartment and the door was locked. I used my key to get in and I met a stronger emptiness. The parlour was as it was but the bedroom was scarce. The wardrobe stood open, no trace of her scent, she did not scrub the house of its materials alone, but washed out her smell. Janet was gone, all this happened two years ago and I have not set my eyes on her ever since then. She was not from this part; all efforts to find her have thus far failed. And I never asked for her last name, her first name I searched on Facebook did not match her face. I did not even know how far to look, I never knew her relatives; I was her closest family here. Bello, I had a precious gold and I melted it with coal, and poured it in the ocean. Nature is punishing me for my sins through Efemena for what I did to my angel. I am done for, how long will I continue like this? I feel like a ghost walking on earth with a borrowed body. Help me, my friend; can you help me find meaning in this vague existence of mine?"

Jamuike's head slumped on the table; Mr Bello settled the bills, helped him up and guided him into the car and drove home. On the drive home, Mr Bello worried about Mariam's deteriorating condition in the hospital. The abortion had damaged her womb and now threatened her life in the intensive care unit. The doctor, a childhood friend of his wife, had vowed to tell his wife that he had been committing incest with their daughter. He was positive his wife would leave the marriage after she might have killed him.

At home, Efemena clutched her chest like stones were filling fast in her heart. She hurried to the refrigerator and took a gulp from the orange juice. She would apologize to Jamuike when he came back home. She had not been fair as he made efforts to make their marriage work. She closed her eyes and prayed for his safe return. Her mother had told her that: "Even if your spouse has an irredeemable flaw, you remain blind towards the possibilities of it undermining your future with him or her. You are a lover that is oblivious to his or her shortcomings, partiality, infidelity, dishonesty, ego, brutality, questionable love and care, but yet ready to absorb sequential hurts, to give room to come to roost, to give that man or woman a second chance, a second coming into your life, body and mind. But one must get his or her cracks to patch. Before being a wife, or husband, everybody is first human, someone's loved one, and must put feelings first, get aches treated, prevent former pains and be protected from heartbreaks."

❧‖ *Twenty-three* ‖❧

The punch Jamuike gave Efemena must have tightened some loose knot. She stayed at home for three weeks, acting as a good mother to her son, and amiable to Jamuike. They were allies in the good days and it did not cost much to rekindle that atmosphere.

It was a hot Saturday; the family went to a newly opened central park. After a while, Efemena begged Jamuike to take her to the big market so she could negotiate with some clients. They drove through the town and made funny remarks at some scenes on the road. Ifeanyi was excited to see his parents happy and cordial. They told him stories and jokes that made him laugh. Efemena thought of how she would miss this moment though. Her time was up. She thought about her plans and fought the tears threatening to fall. They arrived at the shopping centre and Efemena got out of the car with Ifeanyi while Jamuike looked for a suitable parking space. In no time he was some steps behind them.

Jamuike got closer to see the client Efemena was hugging and greeting at a shop's entrance. Jamuike froze instantly; he almost tripped. He was shocked she was different, refined and more beautiful.

It had been two years that he last saw her–his angel. Her eyes bored into his and he forgot he was there with his family. They stared at each other asking silent questions. Janet had tears in her eyes. Ifeanyi broke the mood. He grabbed his father's polo shirt calling, 'Daddy, Daddy'. Efemena turned to his direction; he grabbed his son's hands, lifted him up on his arm and walked towards them. Efemena cleared her throat as she observed the tense atmosphere between Janet and her husband and wondered if they knew each other.

"Efemena, who is this man?" Janet asked without taking her eyes off Jamuike.

"He is my husband, why?" Efemena responded. She was suspicious.

"Efemena, this is my Jamuike," Janet said softly and broke into tears.

Efemena gathered Janet in her arms, she was crying too. She consoled Janet patting her shoulders. She steered Janet towards the office and sat her down.

"Do not cry, dear, it is okay, everything would be fine. Do not cry, please do not cry."

"Efemena, I … I … I can't hold… hold them," Janet stuttered with her words.

"Hush, I got you, I know," Efemena consoled her.

Jamuike watched from a distance. He felt a strong impulse to kneel beside her and apologize for the pains he had caused her. *"My angel I'm so sorry. Stick every hook in my limbs and I will take each pain that comes from it without regrets. Forgive me, my darling, I will die a thousand times if it can bring back the joy I took from you, please,"* he cried inside.

He carried Ifeanyi playfully though with a heavy heart. Efemena stayed in the office with Janet. Thirty minutes later, she called the sales representative to handle the shop because she was going to take her *madam* home. She wished she could absorb all the anguish of her friend, she felt like knocking Jamuike off, kicking his chin hard for his raw stupidity, her friend loved him like air she breathed. Efemena knew what she had to do. Janet deserved to be happy and she was willing to make her friend smile again.

After service on Sunday, Efemena, Jamuike along with Ifeanyi went to visit Janet. After chatting awhile, they took their leave and promised to call back some other time. Jamuike fidgeted throughout the visit while Ifeanyi became fond of his new aunt.

At night, Efemena called Jamuike severally but he did not respond. She was curious, because she was sure he was in his room, she entered expecting him to be asleep. But she found him awake, sitting on his bed with knees raised high to his chin and his head burrowed deep in it. She sat on the bed beside him and called his name softly as she slowly raised his head up. His crimson eyes stared at her. She could not bear to see him this way. She hugged him and in silence they cuddled each other to sleep.

In the morning, she served him his breakfast in bed. He finished his tea and placed the tray on the table. Efemena started talking.

"Jamuike, the reason why I came here last night was to talk about Janet, but if you are not feeling fine yet, we could talk some other time."

"Efemena, you can talk. I am okay." He smiled weakly. She drew a deep breath.

"Okay. I have known Janet for five years now. I knew her before I was deployed to serve here. She has been my fashion designer. The first time I was here on business, she sewed very nice dresses and shirts for me and since then I needed not come down here. She buys the materials, snaps and I give her the go ahead to make the styles, and afterwards, she sends them to the West.

"When I came around, it made business easier. We became close friends, more like sisters. I know lots of good men have asked tirelessly for her hand in marriage and on every occasion, she turned down their proposals.

"I became worried because she was not getting younger. I

even tried matchmaking few times but she would have none of my meddling. I had wished to be amongst her bridal train or maid of honour.

"I became withdrawn because she refused to hint why she would not consider any suitor. Our relationship suffered, and became business-like until she opened the doors of her heart and told me of her past. She disclosed how marriage held no marital bliss for her.

"She was in love with a handsome promising man. A nice couple they made, all was good until he ditched her. She was pregnant then. He was neither ready to marry nor have kids. His words shattered her to pieces. She took his decision with bravery, didn't tell him of the little one growing inside of her so that he would not think she wanted to trap him. She hid the news from him, and buried the foetus from the world.

"She was two months gone when he made his decision. She waited another month to see if he would come back and refute his non-committal statements. He never came back. She got rid of the pregnancy and decided to wait till he comes back; she could not love anyone else. She was admitted at the hospital for two months due to excessive bleeding, he did not look for her. The abortion ruptured her womb. She would be called a man in her husband's house, ridiculed by the society and shunned by his relatives.

"She grew up in an orphanage. When she came of age, The organization set her business up. She never knew her parents, there was no family to run to or back her up in difficult times. The pain was unbearable moreso she could not bear a child."

Jamuike's sadness was compounded. "Oh my God! I knew none of these."

"Jamuike, Janet is barren; she aborted your baby. When the report showed she could not conceive, she died a thousand times. She knew then she could not wait for you anymore, she loved you too much and could not bear making you childless if you eventually decided to marry her."

"My goodness, I am so sorry. Please, Efemena, I did not know, forgive me, take me to her I beg you."

"Jamuike, when I told you I was going to travel last month, you did not let me say for what purpose. I have gotten admission at a university in Sierra Leone for my master's programme. But now, Jamuike, our son is Janet's."

The meaning of Efemena's last words struck Jamuike. He gathered her in a tight hug, almost squeezing her. He cooped her face tenderly, looked in her eyes and smiled. All was not lost. He could finally find peace.

"I am such a cruel beast, yet, God blessed me with two adorable angels. How graced can a man be? Efemena, I'm forever grateful, you have a pure heart. The sky will be your limit. I promise you this day to work hard and give Ifeanyi and Janet my best. We would visit you when you get there. God bless you, Efemena." They hugged fiercely and rocked like babies who just shared each other's candy as friendship oath.

In the months that followed, Efemena and Jamuike's wedding was dissolved. They made collective plans for her trip. In their scuttle, Janet came around to babysit Ifeanyi, and established a good relationship with her new son.

Twenty-four

Three months into her first semester, she was so happy going through the wedding album of her best friends. She looked at them with contentment. Mr and Mrs Bello stood as Janet's parents, their little daughter Susan the flower girl, while Ifeanyi was a ring bearer. She opened her webcam to call them. They were scheduled for a family chat and she was right on time.

"Hello!" Efemena waved at them smiling. The two waved at her with the same energy.

"Blissful honeymoon, my darlings, wow!" Efemena exclaimed.

"Hi sweet," Janet smiled.

"Hello, my darling. Where is that little champ, can't see him anywhere?" Efemena asked after Ifeanyi.

"Oh, that naughty boy? Jamuike just tucked him in; he would not to go to bed. He was delaying our moment."

"Really, that boy. Why did not you wear him out?" Efemena smiled.

"Trust, dear. I exhaused him with Ninja fights; I would allow him win just to satisfy him. Jamuike was the partial referee."

"Anyway, you should rest. Big hugs and have a good night rest."

"I happily send you off to bed as well," Janet blew Efemena a kiss.

Efemena laughed excitedly. "Janet, flowers must have infiltrated your brains, are you sure you threw your bouquet out to the ladies for it?" she teased.

"Of course, I did. How could I not, naughty you, good night, sweetie. We all love you so much, bye," Janet said.

"Efemena, thanks so much, you are an angel in disguise, you

saved me and brought back meaning to our world, we appreciae you so much, and we hope to plan a vacation next month to be with you," Jamuike replied.

"Yes, Efemena, I seriously look forward to seeing you. I miss you, miss you so much."

"You are welcome, Jamuike, all thanks to God, he is always faithful. Now out, out both of you. And Janet, I will be sending the goods soon; I got some really nice fabrics you would love. Don't be overly excited, and check the mail I sent you. I'm sure you have not done that. It has the details of the goods; please, Jamuike, you are in charge. If her head stays in the moon, get yours back from the clouds and make her attend to business!" The three of them laughed.

"Goodnight, love birds, you guys be good and stay out of trouble." Jamuike and Janet said goodbye and turned off thier computer.

She yawned and thought about the presentation she had at the university by noon the next day. She picked the television remote and changed the channel.

The epidemic Ebola was all over the air with the horrific statement it might have spread to Nigeria by an elite Liberian, who made an unofficial visit he should not have embarked on, aware that the virus was contagious.

She was frantic and decided to call her family. She decided not to disrupt their honeymoon. In the morning she would put a call through so they could take precautions. She called her parents and siblings instead, who had already heard the news. By the next morning, it had hit the streets. Even at Fourah Bay College, it was no news either. Students, those in the sciences and in various faculties, were already enlisting themselves to voluntarily combat the disease and assist health care centres and the Red Cross Society. Efemena enlisted and was committed in her service of providing food and clothes to orphans.

❧‖ *Twenty-five* ‖❧

A year passed and Efemena made a trip home. Ifeanyi was to be a ring bearer for her sister's nuptial and she did not want to miss her son in a suit. Also, she could not miss Akpevwe's marriage for anything in the world. She looked forward to seeing Jamuike and Janet. They had adopted a baby girl; Adora Efemena Akuabia, five months younger than Ifeanyi. She smiled at the thought of the happy reunion that awaited her.

The plane touched the ground at exactly 4:45 pm. The Purser celebrated her birthday. The air hostess gave Efemena a souvenir, she had not been able to eat, she did not have the appetite to eat anything. Jamuike waited at the arrival hall. Janet and the kids were supposed to be with him, Efemena thought. They hugged and pecked as Jamuike carted her luggage. On the road, she asked him why the whole family was not there to receive her. They had about an hour drive to the community, it would have been good to begin homecoming on the road. Jamuike did not respond, he concentrated on his driving. Jamuike did not take the lane home. He drove to the state's teaching hospital. Fear crept in on Efemena.

"Jamuike, what is wrong, why have you brought me here?"

"Efemena," Jamuike called her name. It was then she noticed Jamuike's face, he looked sad, his eyes were sunken into their sockets.

Jamuike placed his head on the steering wheel. She came down to his side and placed her hand on his shoulder.

Efemena followed obediently as he led her into the hospital and took her to a ward. The nurses were covering the body of a patient. Jamuike shut his eyes, they were late.

Efemena walked slowly towards the corpse. She didn't want to imagine anything. The length of the corpse and the shape was similar to hers. She lifted the top of the cloth and screamed "Janet!"

"Too late; she wanted to see you for the last time. The kids have been over at your parents for a month now, your mother stayed awhile. When Janet's time was near, she took them to the West. She has been admitted for weeks. Her last wish was to see you before she died. I'm sorry, Efemena, her breast cancer reached stage three. She was going to die," Jamuike said.

Efemena cried. "No, no!" Her heart ached as she placed her palm to it.

"You could have told me on time, Jamuike, you didn't inform me earlier. I would have b-be-en here to be w-w-with h-her." She fell to the ground and sobbed

Ten months later, Efemena blushed as a new bride. There were guests at the traditional marriage. Efemena had just offered her husband a cup bearing red wine. He drank from the cup leaving no drop and put some naira notes inside.

"Come over here, my darling," he mouthed to her as he watched the elders from her clan approach him; they counted "one, two, three" and with loud cheers from everybody, placed her on his thighs. He wound his arms around her waist possessively.

Efemena whispered into her husband's ear " Baby, you are making me shy, I feel embarrassed." She hid her face by the side of his neck. He laughed and patted her back like a baby. The way he positioned Efemena put her face in the direction most of her immediate family were seated. Enatomare and her sisters laughed at her daughter's discomfort. Her in-laws grinned at her.

Akpevwe led the group of ladies that escorted the bride back into the bedroom, while the elders and both parents finalized the marriage rites. Family and guests proceeded afterwards to the reception that had been arranged.

Epilogue

The red carpet welcomed the guest as they walked into the great hall. There were different people in the hall, men and women from all walks of life. The Abia State Commisioner for Women Affairs also graced the occasion. Efemena made her way to the honourable commisioner. It was the first anniversary of her foundation and she was glad Mrs Adeze Nwabodo kept her words.

Efemena was overwhelmed with joy; for the past months, Mrs Nwabodo had been a source of inspiration and a mentor. She had supported ECF in accomplishing its goals. She had organized the dazzling reception to appreciate her supporters. The Efemena Cancer Foundation was a year old. After Janet's death, Efemena started an organization that campaigned against the spread of breast cancer. Today would mark its first anniversary and celebrate its tremendous success that had saved and prevented many women, young and old from getting infected. It had also raised the awareness of breast cancer making women understand the need to amputate a breast or both when the disease is critical and educating them the loss of breast was not the end of living, but a chance to live for oneself and loved ones.

Efemena turned to her husband. "Thank you, my darling, I wouldn't have done this without you."

Jamuike raised her hands slowly to his lips and kissed her knuckles. "No, my angel, you did it. You're a strong and dependable woman. You have a heart of gold and you are ferociously driven.

"Oh, Obim! But still, I could not have come this far without your love, understanding, wisdom, support and friendship."

"Hush …" He kissed her lips. "Honey, look around this hall, the preparations, guests, and success of the fund raiser. My God! You're exceptional. I love you."

"I love you, too." She moved into his arms and he hugged her tightly.

Their kids ran to them tugging at their clothes. "Mummy, Daddy!" Efemena picked up four years old Eleanor. Her white shawl came off her shoulders, Jamuike held out his hand to Eleanor, and he placed her in his hands.

"Daddy, can we go home now? We are tired!" Eleanor spoke.

"Yes, yes, let us go home, Daddy, Mummy tell Daddy to take us home," They chorused.

Eleanor had become outspoken after Efemena brought her from Liberia. She lost her parents, siblings and relations to Ebola. Efemena and Jamuike showered her with love and care to fill the void of the past.

"I can see you have all held a meeting. Your small minds are made up eh? Okay oh, home-bound we are. Ifeanyi, take your sisters and tell your grandparents that we will leave in less than thirty minutes. Now go, girl." As soon as he put Eleanor down, they took off in a race.

"And easy, easy, you don't want to scratch your knees again. Elea …" His warnings fell on deaf ears.

"Mrs Akuabia, your squad has shortened our stay, and I think I like that. How about we give Ifeanyi a brother tonight?" he winked.

Efemena laughed as she wrapped her hands around his neck. "Jamuike, we have three kids already."

"Yea, I want one more baby: two boys and two girls. Just the way you feed me with balanced diet … in fact, you can give me an overdose of it. I've missed you and can't wait to get all these fineries off your body. Have I told you how gorgeous you look tonight, my angel?"

"Countless times, my love. Let's go home," she whispered into his ears and bit it. He shouted as he grabbed her waist.

"Mr Akuabia, take me home." Jamuike laughed.

"Come on, let's get out of here fast. Ada and others can oversee this event."

"Sure, sweetheart"

✳   ✳   ✳   ✳   ✳

Later at night in their bedroom, Efemena changed into a sexy nightwear Ada had picked for their honeymoon. Jamuike was sprawled on the bed, revealing his chest; he had no underwear on.

"Baby, how long will it take you to walk towards our bed? Come to me, my love, I have longed for this moment ever since I took you as my wife."

Efemena hid her face behind the curtain. "The bulb is too bright, can you put it off, Ike, or dim it, it affects my eyes."

Jamuike smiled. "I know you are shy, but you do not have to be. I have married you in the right way and I will love and cherish you till we grow old. So, relax, babe, and be at ease with your hubby, my darling. Desire filled his voice as he got off the bed. He swept Efemena off her feet and brought her to the bed.

"Jamuike?" she called his name softly.

"Yes, sweetheart." He nuzzled her neck. "Yummy, my baby, you taste so good. I am a lucky man, I shall make you the luckiest amongst women, wives, and of course mothers!"

Jamuike lowered Efemena slowly on the mattress and rested on one knee, placing the other on the floor. She felt his erect manhood and shut her eyes, taking a deep breath. Jamuike's robe served as cover while he made love to his wife in all ways he had promised, with love only for each other.

Kraftgriots

Also in the series (FICTION) *(continued)*

Ibrahim Buhari: *A Quiet Revolutionary* (2012)
Onyekachi Peter Onuoha: *Idara* (2012)
Akeem Adebiyi: *The Negative Courage* (2012)
Onyekachi Peter Onuoha: *Moonlight Lady* (2012)
Temitope Obasa: *Strokes of Life* (2012)
Chigbo Nnoli: *Save the Dream* (2012)
Florence Attamah-Abenemi: *A Bouquet of Regrets* (2013)
Ikechukwu Emmanuel Asika: *Tamara* (2013)
Aire Oboh: *Branded Fugitives* (2013)
Emmanuel Esemedafe: *The Schooldays of Edore* (2013)
Abubakar Gimba: *Footprints* (2013)
Emmanuel C.S. Ojukwu: *Sunset for Mr Dobromir* (2013)
Million John: *Amongst the Survivors* (2013)
Onyekachi Peter Onuoha: *My Father Lied* (2013)
Razinat T. Mohammed: *Habiba* (2013)
Onyekachi Peter Onuoha: *The Scream of Ola* (2013)
Oluwakemi Omowaire: *Dead Roses* (2013)
Chidubem Iweka: *So Bright a Darkness* (2014)
Asabe K. Usman: *Destinies of Life* (2014)
Stan-Collins Ubaka: *A Cry of Innocence* (2014)
Data Osa Don-Pedro: *Behind the Mask* (2014)
Stanley Ekwugha: *Your Heart My Home* (2014)
Yemi Ajagbe: *The Triumph of Childhood Trials* (2014)
Ndubuisi George: *Woes of Ikenga* (2014)
Nwanneka Obioma Nwala: *Wives on the Cross* (2014)
Ebere Ezike: *The Housemaid* (2014)
Emmanuel C. S. Ojukwu: *A Whiff of Kahara* (2014)
Bizuum Yadok: *King of the Jungle* (2014)
Onyekachi Peter Onuoha: *The Fears of Mama* (2014)
Ikenna Nwadike: *The Holy Heist* (2014)
Chukwu Adindu: *Destined Not to Arrive* (2015)
rome aboh: *above the rubble* (2015)
Terhemba Shija: *The Siege, the Saga* (2015)
Emmanuel Iwuno: *The Broken Path* (2015)
Mazi Sam Ohuabunwa: *The Port Harcourt Volunteer* (2015)
Onyekachi Peter Onucha: *Identity* (2015)
Gloria Ernest-Samuel: *Iheoma My Dear* (2016)
Clement Chukwuka Idegwu: *Right to be Angry* (2016)
Ibe Ifeanyi: *The Urashi Conquest* (2016)
Phil Ngozi Nwoko: *Dancing with the Ostrich* (2016)
Aoiri Obaigbo: *The Wretched Billionaire* (2016)
Kaase Fyanka: *The Golden Sword of Dragon* (2016)
Data Osa Don-Pedro: *I am Somebody* (2016)
Jerry Alagbaoso: *Officers and Men* (2016)
Liwhu Betiang: *The Rape of Hope* (2016)

Lola Akande: *What it Takes* (2016)
Zaynab Alkali: *Invisible Borders* (2016)
Liwhu Betiang: *The Rape of Hope* (2016)
Jerry Alagbaoso: *Officers and Men* (2016)
Emmanuel C.S. Ojukwu: *Sugarcane Receipts* (2016)
Tony Nwaka: *Mountain of Yesterday* (2017)
Law Ikay Ezeh: *Your Church My Shrine* (2017)
Oselumhense Anetor: *Triumph of Innocence* (2017)
Orlando Dokubo: *The Arm Twist* (2017)
Chinwe Okoli: *A Daunting Odyssey* (2017)
Femi Adedina: *Highway to Nowhere* (2018)
Lola Akande: *Where Are You From?* (2018)
Ugochukwu Agballah: *Where the Rain Started Beating Us* (2018)

www.ingramcontent.com/pod-product-compliance
Lightning Source LLC
Chambersburg PA
CBHW020116180626
46812CB00006B/2629